UNTIL

DEATH

CYNTHIA
EDEN

PROLOGUE

The giant sea monster flew down the packed city streets. Its tentacles shot high into the air and its bright green body shone beneath the lights. Screams rose in the air, high, desperate cries of —

"Throw me something!"

Ivy DuLane smiled at those cries even as she let loose and threw a handful of gleaming, plastic necklaces into the crowd. The people out there roared even louder as the Mardi Gras parade really kicked into high gear.

Mardi Gras in Mobile. Damn, but she loved these nights. The Royal Ladies of Poseidon were ruling this town. Her float was rocking as it bobbed its way down the busy street. One of the high school bands marched in front of her sea monster, and the band's music drifted into the air, merging with the cries from the crowd.

Ivy paused just a moment to adjust the mask that she wore — everyone on the float was wearing a pale, blue mask just like hers. The blue mask covered her eyes and just skimmed the top of her nose. Ivy swayed with the music and her smile stretched.

Energy pumped into the air. Those screams were full of joy and —

"Help me!"

Ivy's head whipped to the right. She'd just grabbed more Mardi Gras beads from her post, but that cry stilled her hand. Her frantic gaze swept over the crowded street, looking past the barricade that the cops had set up to protect the parade goers.

She saw men and women. Children. They were all talking and laughing. Waving their hands into the air as they tried to catch the throws from the floats.

Behind the crowd, though, darkness waited. Shadows swept away from the street, heading back toward the old buildings. As she stared into those shadows, a shiver swept over Ivy.

The sea monster jerked and her hands flew out as she steadied herself. When the float moved, the crowd parted, just a bit, and she saw the two lovers in the darkness.

The man was behind the woman, one of his arms was wrapped around her waist and his other arm —

A knife glinted in the dark.

They aren't lovers.

"Stop!" Ivy yelled as she dropped her beads and grabbed onto the side of the float.

The float didn't stop. The crowd kept yelling. The band played even louder.

The man — he had on a Mardi Gras mask, too. A mask and a tux, as if he were going to one of the Mardi Gras balls — balls that seemed to occur at a near constant rate during this time of the year. The woman was struggling in his arms, her glittering, gold evening gown twisting with her movements. It was that glittering gown that had caught Ivy's attention. It sparkled so brightly in the dark.

Almost as brightly as the knife in the man's hand.

"*Stop!*" Ivy shouted again. No one was listening to her. "Get away from her!" Ivy yelled to that man out there.

Did he laugh? She couldn't tell for sure. It seemed that he might be staring right at her.

He plunged the knife into the woman's side.

"No!" And the parade float wasn't stopping. The driver down below probably didn't even hear her. No one seemed to hear her.

There was no choice. Ivy couldn't just watch the woman die.

The masked man drove the knife into her side again.

Ivy jumped right over the side of her sea monster. When she hit the pavement, she stumbled to her knees and her palms scraped over the pavement. The crowd gasped, no doubt because the people on the floats weren't supposed to fly off them.

And people in the crowd aren't supposed to be murdered!

Men and women stared at her in shock as Ivy rushed toward the barricades. She had to get to that woman! She had to help her. Voices were rising behind Ivy. Her friends from the float were shouting her name.

"He's killing her!" Ivy yelled back. Then she looked at the crowd. "Let me pass! We have to stop him!"

A horse galloped up behind her. She glanced over her shoulder and saw the mounted police officer. "Help me!" Her plea was desperate as she scaled the barricade that had been put up to separate the spectators from the rolling floats. "I saw a man — he was attacking a woman!"

The cop's face hardened. People nearby weren't watching the parade any longer. They were watching Ivy and the cop. Ivy finally got over that barricade. She raced toward the spot where that poor woman had been, and she —

Empty.

No one was standing there. No man in a white mask. No woman in a gown that glittered like gold.

Ivy spun around, stunned, lost. Where had they gone? And where was the blood? The knife?

"Ma'am…" A cop grabbed her arm. *Not* the cop who'd been mounted on the horse. Another one. A guy wearing a uniform and sporting a shiny badge near his breast pocket. "Ma'am, what the hell are you doing?"

"I —" She looked around again, but a sea of people surrounded her. The parade was still going. One crazy woman jumping from a float hadn't stopped it. Screams and music filled the air. "A woman was in trouble," Ivy tried to explain. "A man was stabbing her."

The cop's hold tightened on her arm. "Have you been drinking?" He brought his face in closer to hers. Probably the better to sniff her for the scent of alcohol.

Her back teeth clenched. "Not tonight, I haven't." She glared at him. "I saw them! We have to find the woman! She needs help."

Music boomed from the street.

"She needs help," Ivy said again as she tried to search through the crowd. "I know what I saw. I know…"

Only there was no victim. There was no attacker. There was nothing.

***

He kept his hand over her sweet mouth. Not that it mattered, not then. She wasn't fighting anymore. Actually, he didn't think she was even breathing.

He and his lovely prey were inside the abandoned building, just a few feet away from the cop and the would-be rescuer.

She still had her mask on, but he could see the heavy mass of her dark hair, falling around her shoulders. She was a small woman, petite, almost delicate, but curved in all of the ways that he enjoyed.

A small woman like her — she wouldn't be able to put up much of a fight.

They never do.

The cop wasn't buying her story. Through the crack in the boarded-up window, he had a perfect view of the cop — and the woman who'd leapt from that float.

I didn't expect that move.

She'd seen him. She'd watched while he'd driven the knife into his victim's tender flesh. No one had watched before.

A little thrill still coursed through him.

She saw me.

But now the uniformed cop was tugging her away from the scene. He was muttering about rich women who drank too much. Everyone knew the people on the floats liked to party during the parade. The cop wouldn't even check the area. He was just walking away and probably heading off to lock up the brunette.

"See," he whispered into the dead woman's ear. "No one gives a damn about you. I was the only one. You should have appreciated me when you had the chance."

He let her slide down his body. She hit the dirty floor, her gown pooling around her. He bent and wiped his knife on that gown, then he pressed a quick kiss to her lips. She tasted sweet, even in death.

The music and laughter kept coming from outside, calling to him. He put the knife back in its sheath and slipped outside. He made sure to secure the back door—it wouldn't do for someone to stumble onto his prize—then he hurried around the side of the building, following the cop and the interesting new lady. His gaze slid to the lady in the blue mask. She was yanking against the cop's hold and demanding that he launch a search of the area.

She was interesting. He'd like to see her without that mask.

His hand lifted and he touched his own mask.

Would you like to see me?

The cop moved faster, the crowd clearing for him. The crowd...they were clueless. You could do so much right in front of them, and they never knew.

He kept to the shadows and he followed that cop and that very interesting new prey.

He hadn't planned to hunt again, not so soon, but this one...this woman was going to be special.

He could feel it, and now, he understood so very much.

I might just let you see me...all of me.

CHAPTER ONE

"Causing trouble again?"

Ivy froze at that deep, rumbling voice. A voice that she usually only heard in her dreams — those really hot ones that came late at night.

"Drunk and disorderly conduct," that sexy voice continued and she could feel tension gathering between her shoulder blades. "And did you seriously jump *off* a float in the middle of a parade? Don't they teach you not to do things like that in manners school?"

She turned away from the uniformed cop — the jerk who was seriously trying to get her into the back of a patrol car — and faced this new threat. Because, yes, that was how she always thought of Detective Bennett Morgan. *Threat. Danger.* But in this instance, he could be her way out. Because if the fresh-faced uniform succeeded in his dumb plan to send her down to the drunk tank, her night was screwed.

"I'm not drunk," Ivy said. There was no way she could keep the heat from her voice. Fury rode her too hard. *A woman was attacked! No one is doing anything!* "I've said the alphabet backwards twice now, I've touched my nose with my fingers a dozen times, and I've walked in the straightest line in the world." Her voice shook with fury. "I saw a woman being attacked. I tried to *help*," she emphasized heavily. "My only crime was being a good Samaritan." And for that, the young cop wanted to toss her in jail. Not cool.

Bennett stalked toward her. A streetlight fell on him, revealing the hard planes of his face. Bennett wasn't traditionally handsome. No, he was far too rough for that. Rough and wild with his thick, slightly long, blond hair and those deep, brooding eyes of his. She couldn't see the emerald green shade of his gaze at that moment, but she'd never been able to forget that color. Bennett's jaw was square, a faint cleft marked the center of his chin, and his high cheekbones gave the guy a wild edge.

An edge that she would *not* be exploring. At least, not right then.

She'd had a rather unhealthy attraction to Bennett since she was eighteen years old. Their time apart — all of those years — should have dimmed that attraction. It hadn't. She looked at him, and that same sensual awareness flared within her.

Don't let him see it. Don't.

She lifted her cuffed hands and she moved closer to him. Bennett might be many things, not all of them good, but he *was* the Mobile Police Department's golden boy of the moment. The big, bad, new hotshot detective who'd come to town a month ago. So maybe the hotshot could assist her. "Bennett, please, talk to the guy. Help me."

His hand brushed down her arm. She hated that his touch seemed to scorch right to her soul. He shouldn't still affect her that way. But he did.

Damn him.

Bennett's gaze raked over her. "Officer Chambliss," he said, referring to the cop who was all too eager to toss her into a drunk tank some place and forget about her. "You know who this woman is, right? Senator DuLane's daughter?"

Her eyes squeezed closed. Was Bennett really trying to ruin her night or what? Now she'd be in jail *and* on the scandal page of the local paper. Mentioning her father wasn't going to help anything. The guy was dead and buried, and before he'd been put in the ground, he'd wrecked more than his share of lives.

Maybe that was why Bennett mentioned him. To remind me that he hasn't forgotten.

Or forgiven.

"Did you give her a breathalyzer?" Bennett asked as he tilted his head to the side.

"Y-yes, of course!" The redheaded cop said quickly.

"Is she drunk?"

"Not legally," Officer Chambliss was forced to admit, "but…you should have seen her dive off that float!"

"I wish I had," Bennett muttered.

Ivy glared at him.

"Someone could've been hurt," the young cop blustered. "Someone could've —"

"If she's not legally drunk, then we can't hold her." Bennett's voice was as mild-as-you-please. "Trust me on this, buddy, you don't want the headache that she will bring your way. Not when you're still new to the force."

She held her breath. Hoping. Praying —

"I'll take care of her," Bennett offered. His badge was clipped to his belt, gleaming dully. Other than the badge, he didn't look like a cop at all. He just wore jeans, a loose shirt, and a rather battered looking coat. "I'll make sure that she doesn't jump off anymore floats tonight."

Officer Chambliss hesitated.

The stupid cuffs bit into her wrists. She was wearing her Royal Ladies of Poseidon outfit, a thin bit of silk and lace that barely skimmed the top of her thighs. Sure, she had on tights, but the get-up was supposed to be seen from the perch of a float, not all up-close and personal. Ivy felt way too exposed, especially with Bennett's gaze raking over her.

"She won't cause any more trouble," Bennett said. "I promise you that."

He shouldn't make promises that he couldn't keep. Bennett didn't know her well, not anymore. She excelled at trouble. She wasn't the good girl he remembered. Not even close.

That girl was long gone. Being good didn't solve problems. Taking risks — finding danger — that was the way to get the job done.

But the uniformed cop nodded and the guy actually freed her from the cuffs. Ivy exhaled on a harsh sigh of relief. It wouldn't have been her first visit to the jail — unfortunately — but she was very glad she wouldn't be returning that night.

"She's your problem now," Officer Chambliss growled then he turned and climbed into the driver's seat of his patrol car.

Ivy glared after him. "I'm not a problem! I'm a person! You aren't any kind of —"

Bennett snagged her wrist and pulled her toward him. "If you antagonize him, you *will* find that sweet ass of yours tossed into the patrol car." His fingers slid over her inner wrist. "Were the cuffs too tight?"

Her pulse raced beneath his touch, and Ivy tried to jerk her hand away. Bennett shook his head and kept his hold on her.

"I have to look for the woman," Ivy told him quickly. "I don't know what you heard about what happened tonight —"

"I heard you jumped off a float."

She rolled her eyes. "I saw a man, okay? A masked man with a knife. He was stabbing a woman who was wearing a gold evening gown."

He kept rubbing her wrist.

"Stop it," she ordered, refusing to be shaken by him or his touch. "This is important! I think — I think the woman may be dead."

He let her go.

Ivy swallowed and tried to settle her nerves. Bennett was the lead homicide detective in the area. If anyone could help her, it would be him. "Please." And she *never* begged him, but she was begging right then. "I'm not crazy. I'm not drunk. A woman was hurt tonight, and I'm afraid he killed her while the crowd just cheered around him."

He searched her face. She stared back at him, her whole body tense.

Then Bennett swore. "Shit. Show me, now."

She nodded quickly and spun on her heel. Bennett would get to the bottom of this nightmare. He was a good cop, even if he did have a tendency to piss her off way too much. Piss her off, turn her on, far too many things that she couldn't think about in that chaotic moment. She'd taken about four steps when he grabbed her and pulled her back.

"Bennett —"

He put a coat around her shoulders. His coat.

She blinked up at him. They were all the way down in Mobile, Alabama, right on the Gulf

Coast, so it wasn't as if they were experiencing arctic conditions, but the night was definitely crisp. She could feel his warmth, clinging to that coat. She could smell his rich, masculine scent wrapping around her.

"You were shivering," he muttered. "Don't make a deal out of this, Ivy."

No deal. She pulled the coat closer and got back to the business of returning to the crime scene. She was actually relieved to have Bennett with her. Until a few months ago, he'd been working with the FBI's Violent Crimes division. She didn't know what had occurred, but he'd left the Bureau abruptly and come back home. Some folks had whispered that he'd gotten burned on his last big case.

She couldn't ever imagine the guy getting burned.

The parade was over, so that meant that the streets had cleared out—ghost town kind of clearing. That was the routine. Parades equaled people packing the downtown area, but as soon as those parades were over, people vanished. They went home, they went into the restaurants, or they hit the balls.

So it was easy to cut through the streets and find her way back to that terrible spot.

"Right here." She paused across from the Square, her gaze on the abandoned building. Historic, beautiful, but now seemingly forsaken. The windows were covered with boards, and the ornate railing on the front of the building was coated with peeling paint. "They were right here. I saw the man. I saw his knife." She whirled toward Bennett. "He stabbed her. I yelled for him to stop. I yelled for help, but no one heard me."

His gaze held hers.

"He had on a mask," Ivy continued quickly. "Like mine, but white." And she could not remember which Mardi Gras society was wearing the white masks this year — but she would be finding out. She wasn't walking away from this situation, no way. *I'm a PI. I can handle this.* So she wasn't a cop with a badge. That didn't mean she couldn't help people. She'd spent the last few years of her life taking cases so that she could *help*.

And atone for the sins of the past.

"His mask covered his full face." It hadn't just been a partial mask like the one she wore. "I didn't imagine what happened. This was real!"

He brushed past her and pulled out his phone. A quick tap on the screen, and a bright light illuminated the scene. *Flashlight app.* "There's no blood," he said.

The cop — Officer Chambliss — had told her the same thing after his big two-second search of the scene.

Bennett kept shining the light. "If someone was stabbed, there'd be —"

He broke off, and his light hit the faint spots on the ground. Spots that had been hit by dozens of shoes as the crowd left the parade. Spots that could be—

"Blood," Ivy whispered.

Bennett glanced at the building. "You say the guy and the victim vanished?"

She nodded.

"If he was dragging an injured woman—or a dead body—he couldn't move very fast. Or very far."

Her gaze cut to the building. "The front door is locked." There was a giant chain and a padlock in front of the main doors and all of the windows on that side were boarded up.

"Then he didn't go in that way." Bennett hurried around to the rear of the building. He slid into the narrow alley way and stopped near a dark door. Bennett reached for the knob, but a quick twist showed that the door was locked.

Dammit. She'd hoped—

"Stand back," Bennett directed.

He lifted his foot and kicked that door open.

Her jaw dropped when the wood splintered. "Wait! Aren't you supposed to have a warrant or—"

He was already rushing inside, his light sweeping the floor. So...*No warrant.* She hurried after him, her steps slower because that darkness inside was so heavy and thick. The place smelled musty and old and when Ivy felt something—

not a rat, not a rat! — race across her shoe, she screamed.

Bennett grabbed her and yanked her against his chest.

Get your control. You're a PI for goodness sake. Act like it.

"Ivy?"

She sucked in a deep breath. "Sorry." She'd panicked. That happened in the dark when *things* were coming at her.

He let her go. His light swept the area once more, flying across the dirty, dusty floor. Yellow eyes gleamed back at them as a rat scurried for cover.

That rat ran right across a pale, slender hand.

Ivy's heart stopped. "Bennett?"

He'd seen the hand, too, and he was already kneeling beside the woman. A woman in a glittering, golden gown. A woman with long, dark hair.

A woman who lay in a pool of blood.

His fingers pressed to the woman's throat, but Ivy already knew they were staring at a dead woman. *I could have saved her! I had the chance...*

Bennett slid away from the body. "Don't touch anything," he ordered, voice curt. 'I'll call this in and get a crime scene team down here."

She wasn't touching anything. She was barely breathing, much less moving. When Bennett's light had fallen on the victim, she'd seen that the woman appeared to be in her mid-twenties. Her face had been chalk-white, her hair thick and dark as it spilled onto the dirty floor.

"All dressed up," Ivy whispered. *And nowhere to go…*

***

They'd found the body. Too fast.

His eyes narrowed as he slid back into the shadows. He'd just left his sweet victim there for a little while. The crowd had thinned, and he'd come back, ready to move his precious prey.

But she wasn't alone.

And all of his plans were about to get *screwed.*

He hunched his shoulders and turned, hurrying down the street. The night hadn't gone at all like he'd planned.

Not at all…

His mask was in his pocket. His fingers slid inside and touched it. He felt so strong when he wore his mask. And his victims knew — he was invincible.

The cops won't stop me. No one will.

Maybe he would show his new prey the mask. She could get up-close to it and then…*then she'll see all of me.*

***

"No!" Ivy snapped at him and, if it had been brighter, Bennett was sure that Ivy's brown eyes would be spitting fury at him. "I'm the one who saw the attack! You don't get to just—just shove me into the back of a car and send me off in the night!"

Sighing, Bennett kept his hold on the patrol car door. "I'm afraid that's exactly what I get to do." Blue police lights flashed around the scene. Reinforcements had come running at his call. Unfortunately, they hadn't come in time to help the victim.

"I *saw*—"

"You said that you saw a man in a white mask. A guy wearing a tux. You couldn't tell me his hair color, his eye color—"

"I told you he was tall," she cut in, her words shooting out fast. "About your height, with broad shoulders. He was fit. Strong."

Since he'd dragged a dead woman into an abandoned building without anyone noticing, it stood to reason that the guy was fairly strong. And as far as being around Bennett's height...*we're looking for a perp who is close to six foot three.*

"I can help!" Ivy told him. "Let me stay."

No way. "The crime scene techs need to work." He inclined his head toward her. "I got your statement, and I'll follow-up with you tomorrow if I have any other questions."

Her jaw dropped. "That's it? I see a murder and you just let me go?"

"What do you want me to do?" He eased closer to her. He had always been drawn to Ivy. "Keep you?" The words hung in the air between them, and he thought about just what he would do if he ever did get to keep the lovely Ivy.

She'd been his first crush, though he doubted she realized it. But then, most of the guys in their class had been drawn to the gorgeous Ivy. It was hard not to look at Ivy and want.

Wide, dark eyes. Full lips. Creamy skin. If Snow White were real and strolling around town, causing trouble, he figured she'd look just like Ivy.

Ivy had high cheek bones, a delicate jaw, and a body that had obviously been built for sin. He'd imagined that body — them together — too many times.

But what he'd *never* imagined, that would be Ivy, tangled up in a murder scene. He should have, though. Especially with all the drama that her family liked to cause.

DuLane Investigations. That particular PI business had been in operation since Ivy's grandfather opened it up back in 1970. It was a business known for attracting scandal and raising serious hell.

"Officer East will escort you home," Bennett told her, aware that his voice had roughened.

Ivy could look for trouble elsewhere. This case was his. "He'll make sure that you arrive safely."

"It's not my safety that we need to worry about," Ivy argued quickly. "I can take care of myself. There's a killer out there! We need to focus on stopping him."

Because he didn't realize that. His hands curled around her shoulders and he pushed her into the back of that car. "You saw the killer," he told her bluntly. "Did you ever stop to think…maybe he saw you, too?"

Bennett heard the quick hitch in her breathing.

That's right. "So, yes, I believe you can protect yourself." He'd seen her at a shooting range before, and he knew she'd gotten her black belt in Tae Kwon Do by the time she was fourteen. "But you're getting a police escort home. It makes me feel better, all right?" He eased away from the car.

Her hand flew out and caught his wrist. Her touch was soft, oddly sensual. "I had my mask on, too," Ivy said quickly. "He won't know who I am."

He will if he lingered. If he watched… Bennett shook his head. "If he was standing in that building while you and the cop were outside before, he could've heard you talking." She needed to understand what she faced. "He could have followed you and watched until you took off your mask *or* until you gave the cop your name." With that information, it would be too easy to track her down. "You're getting a police escort home. Lock your doors. Set your alarm. And I *will* be seeing you tomorrow."

Her hand began to slide away from his. Bennett's hand twisted and he caught her fingers in his. "If you need me, call me."

"I-I don't have your number."

What? Bennett shook his head. Sometimes he forgot…despite the tangled web between them, plenty had changed over the years. He gave her the number, then, just to be safe, he scribbled it down on a piece of paper and tucked it into her hand. "Call me." *Anytime.* "I'll come to you."

Then he made himself pull back. Officer East stood just a few feet away, watching him with wide eyes. He wondered if this was the guy's first murder scene.

If the fellow planned to make a career out of law enforcement, it wouldn't be his last.

Bennett had seen too many scenes to count, but those scenes — they often replayed through his nightmares.

Officer East headed briskly toward the driver's side of the vehicle. Bennett stepped into his path. "Keep her safe."

Bennett's guts were twisted over this case, mostly because…hell, when he'd looked down at that woman's body in the abandoned building, when he'd seen her pale skin and that mass of dark hair, he'd realized —

She looks like Ivy.

Same hair color. Same build. An unease had settled heavily around his shoulders.

Officer East nodded and slipped into his car. Bennett watched that patrol car vanish, and he couldn't help but remember another time when Ivy had been taken from him.

Years ago. Another car, another place.

That had been the day he broke Ivy DuLane's heart.

Stay with me, Bennett. I love you.

Her words had haunted him for years. And finally, those words…they'd brought him back home.

But now that he'd finally talked to her again, finally stared into her eyes, he wondered if he'd just followed that dream far too late.

***

Ivy didn't live far from the murder scene — and maybe that should have made her nervous. If the killer had learned her name, then getting her address would be child's play. *And he could easily access my home.*

"Ma'am?" Officer East turned to stare at her. "You want me to come inside with you?"

She glanced at the house. Far too big and rambling. Far too many spaces in there that would make perfect hiding spots. "You're damn right I want you in there." She'd inherited the house when her grandfather died. Part of the place had been renovated and was completely livable — the other part? Not so much.

Ivy remained in the foyer while the cop searched her house. She pulled her coat closer — *Bennett's coat.* She'd forgotten to give it to him before she left the scene, but he'd said that he would see her the next day, so she could always return it to him then. She'd return it and grill him about the case. Because if that guy thought she was just walking away from this situation, he needed to think again.

"Clear."

The cop's voice made her jump. He'd done one very fast sweep of the house and the guy stood near her door now, looking eager to leave.

"Thank you," Ivy told him.

Officer East just nodded, and a few moments later, he was gone. She locked the door behind him, then hesitated, hating that heavy silence around her. Normally, she actually liked the quiet. It let her think. But right then...

A glittering gown soaked with blood. A woman on the floor, blood around her.

Ivy hadn't been able to do a thing to save the other woman.

She turned away from the door, walked through the foyer, and headed for the stairs. Bennett had told her to set her alarm, but she didn't actually have one of those in the house. Not yet. She'd be making an alarm system an immediate priority, though.

She'd only taken a few steps up the stairs when her doorbell rang. The long, loud peal echoed around her. Frowning, her gaze cut back to the door. Had the cop forgot something? She hurried back to the entrance and her fingers fumbled as she unlocked it. Then she hesitated. Surely...if the killer had tracked her down...he wouldn't just ring the doorbell...would he?

Someone pounded on the door. "Come on, Ivy, open up."

Relief had her shoulders sagging. She knew that voice. It was her friend, Cameron Wilde. She finished unlocking the door and she swung it open—

A tall, broad-shouldered man stood on her porch. A well-cut tux covered his body and a white Mardi Gras mask hid his face.

"Hello, Ivy," Cameron said from behind his mask. The sight of that mask chilled her. "Are you ready for a night you won't forget?"

Her porch light glared down on them as she backed up, her heart racing.

CHAPTER TWO

Ivy grabbed the door and tried to shove it closed, but his fingers curled around the wood.

"Uh, Ivy?" he said. "If you don't want to go to the ball, that's—"

The ball? Ivy let go of the door and grabbed his mask.

Cameron Wilde blinked at her. Even under the harsh light, he was perfectly handsome. Perfectly styled. His blond hair swept back from his high forehead, giving him an even more polished look.

"I thought you were changing out of that outfit," he said as his gaze slid over her body. "But if you want to go straight to the ball in—"

"Your Mardi Gras ball is tonight."

"Right." His brows climbed. "That's why we had a date, remember?" Now he sounded annoyed. "That would be why I did that whole 'night you won't forget' bit before."

She stared down at the white mask she now gripped in her hands. It was exactly like the mask that the killer had worn. And Cameron—

he was about the right height. His shoulders were broad and strong.

With the mask on, and with him wearing that tux...Cameron looked just like the killer.

Only Cameron wasn't a killer. She'd known him since she was six years old. They'd been lovers just once — one desperate night — and friends for so long that she could barely remember her days without him.

And yet...as she stared up at him...a shiver slid down her spine.

When I opened the door, it was as if the murderer was standing right before me. Ivy edged back toward her house.

"Ivy? What's wrong?" Then Cameron laughed. "Why are you looking at me like I'm some kind of killer?"

Because I'm trying to figure out if you are. But she didn't tell him that. Instead, she asked, "D-do all of the men in your organization wear these white masks?"

"Those are the ones we picked this year." He shrugged. "I didn't ride in the parade tonight, so I'm not in costume."

Each year, she knew members switched up and different folks would ride in the floats so that all organization members would eventually have a chance to be in a parade. The man she'd seen that night — he'd been in a tux and a mask, just like Cameron's. *Because he's in the same Mardi*

Gras society? Because he was one of the men not riding in their parade?

Cameron was in the Order of the Pharaohs, one of the oldest groups in Mobile. They'd paraded right before her group, kicking off the night. Their ball was already rolling, no doubt packed out and...

Is the killer there?

Because it made sense. Maybe he'd been planning to attend the ball with the woman in the gold gown. But he'd killed her instead. Would he now show up there, just to give himself some kind of alibi?

"Are we going to the ball?" Cameron asked. "Remember the plan, we hit your party, then my ball? Double the fun in one night?" When she didn't respond, his face hardened. "Ivy, what's happening?"

Trust him. She shouldn't be afraid of Cameron, but she was. Because he was the right size and that mask...she thrust it back into his hands. "Where were you earlier tonight?"

He motioned behind him, and she saw the limo idling by the curb. At his cue, the door opened, and another man in a black tux waved toward her. Only he didn't have on a mask.

Her twin brother smiled up at her. "Come on, Ivy!" Hugh yelled. "Don't take all night."

"I was with your brother," Cameron said.

A woman's laughter filled the air.

"And his date," he added. "Shelly." He leaned in closer to her. "Now why don't you tell me what's going on? Why the hell are you looking at me as if you don't even know who I am?"

"I saw a murder tonight," she whispered.

"What?"

Order of the Pharaohs. "And I want to find that killer." She spun on her heel. "Give me five minutes."

She had a ball to attend.

Because the killer might be there...and if he is, I want to find him.

***

Ivy DuLane was trouble. Always had been, for as long as he could remember.

Did she really think no one would notice her? The damn woman couldn't go any place without being noticed.

Bennett put his hands on his hips and glared up at the escalator. Its occupants were slowly descending to the ground level of the convention center, a line of women in their designer dresses and men in their tuxes — with tails. The men had perfectly knotted bow ties. The women had dresses that fit like gloves.

And right in the middle of that crush, wearing a green gown with a slit that exposed far too much of her gorgeous leg...was Ivy.

She was supposed to be home, safe!

Instead, she was walking right into danger, and damn if the woman wasn't on the arm of a bozo wearing a white mask. A mask that far too many other men at that ball were also wearing.

As soon as she reached the ground level, Bennett stalked right toward her. Fury pumped through him. Did she think this was all some kind of game? The woman was crazy, way out of her league.

He stepped into her path.

Her eyes widened. Eyes now lined with shadow and mascara. Eyes that looked even darker than he remembered.

"Hey, buddy," the guy in the mask began. "You need to step—"

"Cameron," she said smoothly, "you remember Bennett Morgan."

Cameron? Oh, hell, *not* Cameron Wilde.

"Ben?" Cameron's golden eyes glinted behind his mask. "Almost didn't recognize you, buddy!"

I'm not the one wearing a mask. And I am not even close to being your buddy.

Cameron slapped his hand on Bennett's shoulder. "It's been too long."

Actually, Bennett rather thought it hadn't been long enough. "She shouldn't be here."

Over their shoulder, he spotted the other couple. Ivy's twin brother Hugh and a curvy redhead. Hugh didn't look overly happy to see him. Not surprising, really. Hugh had once ordered him to stay the hell away from his sister.

Bennett *had* stayed away, for a time.

But he was back, and everything was about to change.

He reached for Ivy's hand. "When I send you home with police protection, you're supposed to stay home." He walked right around to the other escalator — the one that would take her back up to the second level and away from the crush of people. "You're not supposed to just stroll in here and —"

"You think the killer might be here, too, right?" Ivy asked.

For an instant, his eyes squeezed closed. Maybe he should have anticipated that she'd show up there. It had really only been a matter of time before she connected the guy's white mask with the Order of Pharaoh's ball.

Bennett had made the connection as soon as she told him about the mask, and he'd known that he *would* be scouting around that ball scene.

"When I saw Cameron's mask, I knew the guy could be here tonight," Ivy added.

His eyes snapped open. "And, what?" Bennett growled. "You thought you'd use yourself as bait here to lure out the killer?"

She blinked at him. "Oh, jeez, I hope not. I just thought I could look around and see if I saw any guys who matched his description." She motioned to Cameron, and — as pretty much always — the guy bounded to her side.

Some things never change.

"You know identities are supposed to be kept secret in the societies," she said.

God save him from this lunacy...Yes, he knew that.

"But since Cam is in the society, I thought he could identify anyone I saw — you know, men who fit the killer's description. And when I knew who they were, I was going to call you." She smiled at him. A big, wide grin that flashed the dimple in her left cheek. "Because, you know, I have your number."

This had to stop. Absolutely stop. He felt like she was driving him to the edge of sanity.

His hold tightened on her. "You aren't a cop."

Her smile dimmed a bit. "I don't remember claiming to be one. I *am* a PI, though. And private investigators...*investigate*. It's kind of what we do. We don't just sit at home and wait for someone else to solve all the crimes."

Bennett could actually feel his blood pressure rising. "That woman was stabbed, Ivy. Again and again."

She swallowed. "I know that."

Cameron put a comforting hand on her shoulder. Bennett wanted to shove that hand away. Instead, he said, "This isn't some game." He looked at their group in disgust. "You're all in way over your heads, and it's time to go home. The party's over."

Hugh squared his shoulders. "I have a ticket to this ball. Do you, Detective?"

No, but he had his badge, and that would damn well be good enough.

"The only place I'm going," Hugh continued, "is to get Shelly a drink." He lifted the redhead's hand and kissed her knuckles. "Shall we, my love?"

And the guy just strode away with his date, totally ignoring Bennett's orders.

His eyes narrowed as he glared after Ivy's twin. *Mental note…*Hugh was still an asshole.

And that left…

He focused on Ivy and Cameron. The couple most likely to wind up married, only they weren't married. At least, some people had sure thought that. But those people had been wrong.

So was I.

"Ivy," he began.

"I can't get her out of my head," Ivy said, her voice both soft and sad. Her smile was gone now. "I just wanted to look — I *needed* to look around. I was already scheduled to come to this ball, and when I figured out the link…*Bennett, she was wearing her ball gown.* She was supposed to be here tonight!"

Yes, that was why he had officers canvasing the convention center. That was why *he* was there. "I figured that out. I don't need Nancy

Would-Be Drew helping me run my case."
Especially when that help would just put her in
danger. "Go home," he ordered.

"Just let me look around!" She obviously
wasn't backing down. Same old Ivy.

Cameron pressed closer to them. "I don't
like the way you're talking to Ivy."

And he didn't like the way that the guy was
so close to her. They could both just be unhappy.

"I'm the only witness, remember?" Ivy
pushed. "I'm here, let me look."

Dammit...fine. *She was the witness.* And as
much as he wanted to do it, he couldn't
physically carry her out. The PD wouldn't go for
that. "You stay at my side. Every single moment,
got it? We look, but we look together."

Her smile flashed again. "Thank you!"

"And Cameron..."

The guy's brows climbed.

"You know everyone in the society?"

"I do," he said at once, "but...you should
realize anyone could have bought that mask.
They're sold at every party shop in town." He
waved his hand to the thick throng around
them. "And you can rent a tux from dozens of
shops. Get a ticket, get your tux...and boom,
you're set."

Bennett knew that. With Mardi Gras season
hitting hard, everyone seemed to be sporting a
mask of some kind, and that kind of anonymity
just worked to help the perp keep his identity

hidden. The mayor was already freaking out. Murders during Mardi Gras were not good business, and he'd ordered Bennett to this ball before the ME had even loaded the victim's body into the van.

The mayor was hoping Bennett would see something there tonight that would help him. And maybe...with Ivy at his side, he just might.

"I'll go join Hugh for that drink," Cameron muttered. "When you need me, Ivy, come find me at the ice sculpture. The one of the giant Sphinx."

Bennett knew that sculpture—he'd seen it a few minutes before. It was the one next to the whiskey table...the free booze rolled nearly all night long at the balls.

Mardi Gras balls were always popular—too popular. This particular event was one of the biggest, with over four thousand tickets sold. The mayor had been the one to glumly tell Bennett that news. And since no names were taken down when the tickets were sold, he was looking at a pretty giant suspect pool.

Cameron inclined his head to Ivy then vanished into the crowd.

She stared at Bennett.

He tried to yank his gaze from her.

"We're not together," she blurted. "Cameron and I aren't an item or anything like that."

He shook his head. "I didn't ask." But he'd sure wanted to.

"Cameron and I are friends, nothing more. He needed a date, and in a weak moment, I agreed. Then when he showed up at my door tonight, wearing that tux and mask…" For an instant, fear flickered in her gaze. "I was scared of him. I thought—"

That the killer had found her.

His fingers slid down and curled around hers. Not keeping her hand captive any longer, but now, almost caressing her.

"You kind of stick out," Ivy told him, her mouth hitching into a half-smile. "You're the only man here not wearing a tux."

No, he didn't have on a tux. He was wearing his jeans and loose shirt—he'd been off-duty when he first saw her getting pushed toward the back of the patrol car. Hell, how long ago had that been? The night was moving at super speed, and he was struggling to catch up. His left hand tapped against the badge he'd clipped to his belt. "This is the only thing I needed to wear in order to get inside." Besides, his men were there, too. In police uniform, not tuxes.

"Let's start searching," she said briskly.

He nodded, but he wasn't holding out much hope. The mayor had ordered him there, all right, but it wasn't as if a bright shining light would just fall on their perp.

In that crush…finding him would be a miracle. Too bad he'd stopped believing in those long ago.

Back when he'd lost Ivy.

***

They were fools. Drunk, stupid prey. The women swayed in their ridiculously high heels and barely breathed in their skin-tight dresses. His gaze swept over them all, hating them. The men were no better. Too loud. Too drunk.

Too easy to kill.

He took a drink of the whiskey and let it slide down his throat, barely feeling that burn as his fingers lifted to touch the ice sculpture right next to him. His hand trailed along the Sphinx, and he smiled.

"Cameron," he murmured to the man who'd just appeared next to him. "Buddy, it's been too long…"

Cameron, still wearing his mask, turned toward him and smiled.

Too easy.

"You've got to tell me…just who is that gorgeous woman I saw on your arm a few moments ago?"

Cameron's smile stretched even more. "Ah, you've got to be talking about Ivy…"

Ivy. He liked that name.

"Ivy DuLane." Cameron downed his whiskey in a quick gulp and motioned for another glass. The whiskey was poured into the ice sculpture — it slid around the tube inside and then fell into Cameron's glass, coming right out of the Sphinx's mouth. "I'll be sure to introduce you later."

Oh, I'd like that. "But it looked as if you lost her..." He gave the other man a commiserating glance. "She ran off...?"

With the cop. He'd seen the badge and he'd realized that trouble had come his way.

Cameron laughed, not seeming even a little offended. The guy was talking way too freely. Maybe because of the drinks. Maybe because he was just an overconfident fool.

"Ivy's just—" Cameron stopped. "She's chatting with an old friend. No harm, no foul."

An old friend who happened to be a cop.

He lifted his whiskey. Downed it fast. And kept his eyes on Ivy.

Hello, lovely. We're going to have so much fun together.

Because she wasn't like the others. He didn't think there would be anything easy about her. *About time.*

***

"It's not like I'm a civilian, you know," Ivy muttered as she pushed her way through the crush of bodies at the ball. Her gaze slid to the left and to the right. There were more men in white masks all around her. But that one was too thin...that one was too short... "Or did you forget that I obtained my PI's license when I was twenty-one?" That whole Nancy Drew line of his had seriously grated. Her grandfather had run DuLane Investigations for over fifty years, and she'd been eager to take up her place at his side.

Then the whole world had come crashing down on her.

But she'd built that world back, piece by piece. *Without Bennett.*

"I haven't forgotten anything about you," Bennett said softly.

His words pulled her gaze toward him. "And I didn't forget you." Despite her best efforts. She'd tried to move the hell on, but it was hard — especially when your heart was buried in the past.

"I have to know something." His voice rumbled as he kept staring at her with that heated green stare of his. "It's not the right time, not the right place..."

No, because they were supposed to be looking for a killer.

"But do you hate me, Ivy?"

Her lips parted in surprise, and she gave a hard, quick shake of her head. "Of course not! I could never hate you."

Some of the tension seemed to ease from his shoulders.

"Why does it matter how I feel?" Ivy asked him, driven to know this.

"Because you matter. You always have. You always will."

Shock rolled through her.

Bennett glanced away from her. "Let's check the ballroom."

Wait—that was it? No more personal sharing? Now they were on to the ballroom? She shook her head and followed after him. He'd better not try to play his mind games with her. She wasn't the game playing type. He'd learn that fact, very soon.

They were in the area known as the "back hall", a long stretch full of tables and makeshift bars. The drinks were free and flowing heavily in this section, and they had to dodge the bar lines in order to gain access to the darkened ballroom.

Once they got into the main ballroom, she saw a band performing on the stage—music blared out, echoing through the cavernous room. Disco lights swept the scene every few moments. As heavy as the crush had been in the back hall, attendance was pretty sparse in that ballroom.

There were several hundred tables set up in the area, and some caterers were preparing the food, but after being in the madness of the back hall, this place—and its relative peace—was almost a relief.

"When we find out the victim's identity, then we'll be closer to knowing our killer," Bennett said.

She nodded, knowing his words were true. Her shoulder brushed against Bennett. "There," she said, pointing to the man in the white mask who was standing to the side, no date in sight. "He's the right height, the right weight…"

And he seemed to be looking right at her.

Actually, he was striding toward her as she watched him.

She felt Bennett tense against her.

The man in the mask was closing in fast. "Hello, there…" The guy's voice hitched up, sounding a bit on the drunk side. "Want to dance?" He offered his hand to her.

Bennett moved in front of her. "No, she damn well doesn't," he said immediately. "Who the hell are you?"

The guy in the mask weaved. "No names…" His eyes crinkled a bit behind the holes in his mask. "That's how it works."

"The hell it does," Bennett fired back.

Um, the plan had been for Cameron to identify potential suspects. Bennett didn't need —

Bennett snatched the mask right off the guy.

Ivy's lips parted in surprise as she found herself staring at Laxton Crenshaw, a city councilman. And he was glaring at Bennett.

"You don't touch me," Laxton said, and he surged toward Bennett, fumbling for the mask. "No one touches me!"

Bennett side-stepped the guy's lunge and Laxton fell to the floor.

The scent of booze drifted off the councilman, nearly burning the air around them. Laxton tried to get up, but he just fell right back down.

From the corner of her eye, she saw Bennett motion with his hand, and a uniformed cop rushed over. *One of his men.*

"Councilman, I'm going to need to know where you were earlier tonight..." Bennett said.

The councilman flipped him off, then he fell back on the floor, laughing.

"That's not a very good alibi," Ivy pointed out.

Laxton's laughter faded. He glanced toward her. His smile turned a little cruel.

He's the right size. And he'd sure zeroed in on her. Could he be the killer?

"We're going to need to escort the councilman out," Bennett told the uniformed cop. "I think he may have overindulged tonight."

And she knew exactly what Bennett was doing. He was going to take the councilman away under the drinking-too-much ruse and grill the guy. Good technique, she had to give him that and—

The music died. The disco lights flashed off. The overhead lights that had been muted to a faint glow also suddenly disappeared.

The only illumination in the ballroom came from the sputtering candles that lined the tables.

"What the hell?" Bennett demanded.

A loud, shrieking alarm pierced the darkness.

Then people started running. Nearly stampeding as they rushed toward the ballroom's exit doors — doors that just led to the overflowing back hall.

Shouts and cries filled the air.

What is happening? Someone jostled into Ivy, hitting her hard, and she spun around.

"I've got you." Warm, strong hands closed around her shoulders and pulled her up against a body. Not just any body — Bennett. His arms wrapped around her as he held her close. "Officer Abrams, get the others to help this crowd! We need to find out what's happening."

"Fire alarm," Ivy said. That was what it sounded like to her. And everyone was seriously panicking as they fought for freedom.

Bennett swore. "Come on, let's get you out of here."

"I'm okay." She was. But she could hear people crying out in pain and fear as they trampled each other in their fear. "Go, do your job. Help them."

His hold tightened on her.

"I can get out." She knew this place. "Go."

She didn't even know where the councilman had fled to — the guy had vanished in that darkness. A big crowd was near the doors, people shoving and bottling up there as they fought to get out of the main ballroom.

She could see the outline of those bodies in the sputtering candlelight. The alarm kept shrieking from overhead.

"*Go,*" Ivy told Bennett again. He didn't need to worry about her, but—

He started half-dragging, half-carrying her to the right. Away from the doors and toward the stage.

"Bennett? Stop!" Ivy ordered him. "You—"

He pushed her toward the stage. "Take the door behind it. There's a flight of stairs to the right. Those stairs will take you down to the parking garage."

So he knew the building well, too.

"Get outside and get to safety," Bennett said. Then he—

He kissed her.

She didn't expect the kiss, and she wasn't sure he'd even planned that move. His mouth just locked down on hers, hard and fast and devastating. With the alarm shrieking around them. With people screaming.

He kissed her.

And the years fell away. She remembered what it was like to get lost in him. To feel the touch of his mouth on hers and to ignite. She'd always wanted him so wildly, so fiercely, and the years hadn't changed that desire. If anything, now she seemed to want him more.

But he pulled back. "When you're clear, wait for me in front of the convention center. I'll find you there."

Then he was gone. For an instant, Ivy just stood there.

She didn't smell smoke. Didn't hear the crackle of any flames. All she heard was the shriek of the alarm.

The door he'd pointed out waited just a few feet away. But was she really supposed to just take that exit and run? What about Cameron? What about her brother? What about Shelly? They were trapped in the crowd.

I can't leave them.

She wouldn't do it.

***

Chaos. It was all such beautiful, lovely chaos. Women were screaming. Drunk men were fighting each other as they tried to rush out of the building.

There was no fire. There was no danger. Well, none except for the danger that the fools were causing to each other.

He'd set off the alarm. He'd shut down the lights. He'd done it all—in just mere moments.

"Ivy!" Cameron was yelling her name. Cameron and another man — Hugh — were searching for her.

He'd seen Ivy go into the main ballroom. She hadn't come out. Not yet.

Cameron and Hugh would never get to her, not in that mad crush. At least, they wouldn't get to her — not if they kept trying to fight through the crowd. *They need to go another way.*

A way that he knew…

He opened a door, one that had been carefully hidden behind a black curtain. The door took him into a narrow corridor. A service area. The corridor would lead him right to the main ballroom. Right to Ivy.

But he had to hurry. The beautiful chaos would only last so long…

I want to see her. I want to touch her.

He closed the door behind him. The corridor was pitch black, but he had a light. He was prepared.

Always.

He took a few steps. And then he heard someone running toward him. Someone running too fast. His light hit on the man just as the guy barreled toward him.

CHAPTER THREE

She didn't run for the exit that Bennett had showed her. Ivy just couldn't leave her brother and her friends. Instead, she raced for the service corridor. She knew exactly where that corridor was — after all, she'd come to enough parties at that convention center to more than know her way around the place. Besides, her friend Sarah was a caterer who often had her staff working in the service corridor, and Ivy had seen them in action plenty of times. Other people might not know about that secret hallway, but Ivy was just grateful right then that she knew of its location.

A long, black curtain hid the entrance to the service corridor. She shoved the curtain aside and yanked open the door. Darkness waited inside, but Ivy knew that narrow hallway would take her past the thick throng and allow her to exit near the escalators.

Then I'll find Hugh. I'll get him and Cameron and Shelly and we'll all get out.

She ran forward, hating that dark, and she pulled out her phone. She had a flashlight app, too, and she swiped her phone over the screen, turning it on so that she could see —

A man in a tux. A man in a white Mardi Gras mask.

Her breath left her lungs in a startled *whoosh*. She stepped back.

Her light still hit his mask.

"Hello…" His voice was deep, seeming to surround her.

She shook her head. In the middle of a fire — in the middle of mad panic — you didn't just stop to tell someone "Hello".

"You saw me," he continued in that deep voice.

Ivy backed up a step. *Oh, hell, oh, hell…*

"And I saw you."

It's the killer! He had been watching her when she'd been on the float, screaming to get that poor woman help.

She forced her body to relax. If he was about to attack her, he'd find that she wasn't the prey he'd thought. He was bigger than she was, stronger, but that didn't mean he was a better fighter.

"I also saw your brother," he told her. "Such a shame…"

Icy tendrils of fear wrapped around her heart. *He knows about my brother?* "What did you do?"

He turned away from her and began walking back down the hallway. Her light hit the back of his head. He had dark hair, hair that contrasted sharply with the white elastic of his mask's straps.

"What did you do?" Ivy yelled. She raced after him. She grabbed his shoulder and spun him around. When she did, he hit her, hard, slamming her against the wall. Her phone fell from her fingers and crashed into the floor.

His fingers locked around her throat. She felt the slide of gloved fingers tightening around her neck.

Oh, hell, no.

She drove her knee into his groin, hitting him as hard as she could. He swore and his hold eased. *That's right.* Then Ivy whacked him with her elbow, slamming it into his stomach. When he bowled over, she zipped around him. She took a few frantic steps down that hallway —

And then she tripped. Ivy fell over something — something warm and soft.

Not something…someone.

"No," Ivy whispered even as the masked man's words rang in her head. "*Such a shame…*"

Her hands touched something sticky and wet and she shuddered. *Blood.* She knew exactly what blood felt like in the dark.

She was touching a man's body. A man who was wearing a tux and who'd been attacked.

Laughter floated around her. "You're going to be far more fun that I realized."

The hell she was. "This isn't a game!" She backed away from the body. She needed to get away and get help. *Don't be Hugh on the floor. Please, not Hugh.* "The cops are here! They're going to get you—"

"I know they're here." He didn't sound worried. "I saw them and you, sweet Ivy."

He knows my name.

"I can be good to you," he said.

She was on her feet now. Her hands pressed to the wall. Did he brush by her? It was pitch black in there, but she thought she'd felt him. He'd been heading toward the body.

So I need to move the other way. She needed to head back out the way she'd come.

If she couldn't see, then neither could he. Maybe he thought she was down there next to the body. She inched away. She'd get out. She'd go back the way she came and escape. Everything would be okay.

I touched blood…that means he has a knife. Or some kind of weapon.

"I'm going to learn your secrets," he told her. "Your desires. I'm going to give you everything that you ever wanted."

You'll give me nothing. She didn't say those words. Talking would give away her location. She wasn't going to do that. His voice told her that he wasn't close to her. She just needed to keep going. She had to move silently.

"I can be good to you," the killer said. "Or, Ivy, my dear…I can be very, very bad…"

All you can be is crazy. She crept down the corridor. Surely she was close to the ballroom again. She would get away, find the cops—find Bennett—and then this guy would be done.

Only…she stilled. He'd stopped talking, so she didn't know where he was. *He could be right behind me now.*

There was no time to waste. She ran for the ballroom. Forget being quiet—she raced forward.

And the lights flashed on. So bright and glaring after the darkness. She blinked, trying to adjust to that glare, and then she spun around, frantically searching behind her.

He wasn't close to her. He was on the other side of that corridor, near the exit that led to the escalators.

He shoved open the door—

"No!" Ivy screamed.

But he was gone.

And he'd left her…left her with…

Her gaze fell to the floor of that corridor.

A white mask lay near the fallen man's hand.

He left me with a dead man.

***

The convention center's alarm had finally stopped shrieking. The lights were back on and the people in the crowd weren't crushing each other any longer. Bennett saw the men and women blearily staring at each other. They moved slowly now, as if trying to figure out what in the hell was happening.

I'm trying to figure out that one, too.

His men had fanned out into the crowd. There were injured people there — people who'd been trampled near the door. People who'd fallen and would need medical assistance.

Masks were on the floor. Broken Mardi Gras necklaces littered the area.

"It must have been some prank, Detective," one of his team members told him, a detective named Drew Trout. "The building supervisor said someone got into the control room and messed with all the switches there."

And caused panic.

Fear.

A man in a white mask?

He glanced back toward the ballroom. Ivy should be clear by now. The fear eating at him should've eased, but it hadn't.

He needed to see her.

More emergency personnel flooded into the area. Security guards were on scene. And EMTs were already moving into the crowd. He knew that — at events like this one — emergency personnel were always close so that they could respond in an instant.

Like they're doing right now.

He turned and headed back to the ballroom. Chairs were overturned in there, tables tipped onto their sides. Food had been stomped into the flooring.

The ballroom was nearly empty, though.

No sign of Ivy. He headed over to the stage, then he went to that back door. A door that should have given Ivy an easy way out. He grabbed for the handle.

Locked.

His heart slammed into his chest. He yanked harder on that handle.

Locked.

Maybe Ivy had locked the door when she fled. Maybe it had closed and sealed up behind her or —

Maybe she never got out that door because it was locked the whole damn time.

He spun around. "Ivy!" Her name came from him as a roar. "Ivy!"

***

He's not dead, not yet.

She could see the faint rise and fall of the man's chest — not just any man, but a guy she knew.

Councilman Laxton Crenshaw was on the floor of that corridor, bleeding out. Ivy rushed back to his side, and she fell to her knees as she tried to inspect his wounds. He'd been stabbed—multiple times—and the blood was covering his white cummerbund. She put her hands on his chest, trying to stop the blood flow from the worst wound.

His hand flew out and locked around her wrist. "You—"

"He's gone," Ivy told him. "Just stay calm, okay?" He was bleeding so much. Gushing out. "It's going to be all right." Her words could be a total lie, but she didn't care. Weren't you supposed to reassure the victim in situations like this one?

His fingers fell away.

She tried to staunch the blood flow, but the wounds were so deep.

"Help!" Ivy screamed. She was afraid to leave him—if she didn't keep applying pressure, would he bleed out right there? "Help!" And if she didn't go...was he just going to die anyway?

***

Ivy wasn't in the ballroom. He didn't see her in the back hall. Bennett didn't see—

"Ivy!" Hugh DuLane bellowed, running around frantically near the escalators. "Ivy, where are you?"

Bennett's gaze jerked toward the other man. Hugh was a lot of things — not all of them good — but the man had always been fiercely protective of Ivy.

"She's not in the ballroom," Bennett shouted back. "We need to check outside and see if — "

A black curtain parted a few feet away and he saw the door that had been hidden behind it, a door that had just been opened by…Ivy?

She stood there, wearing her gorgeous green dress, and he saw the blood on her. Blood on her stomach. On her hands. Even on her leg.

For an instant, the whole world seemed to stop for Bennett.

"Help," Ivy said, her voice sounding hoarse. *The bastard found her. He hurt her.*

Bennett was already bounding toward her.

"*Help!*" Ivy screamed.

Heads whipped toward her, but she was already running back through that doorway and racing into the corridor there. He rushed after her, yelling her name, but she didn't stop.

Then he saw why.

Ivy fell to her knees beside the prone figure of Laxton Crenshaw.

The blood was his. It was his!

"Help me!" Ivy demanded. She was putting pressure on the councilman's wounds.

Bennett dropped right beside her. Others were rushing into the corridor. "Get an ambulance!" Bennett bellowed when he saw

Detective Trout following him. Then he helped Ivy.

Thank Christ…the blood isn't hers.

But the killer had been there, and he'd left another victim in his wake.

***

He didn't usually like to attack men. It wasn't as much fun with them. Their skin didn't cut as easily, the blade didn't slide right in for them.

The thrill wasn't the same. The release was different, less fulfilling.

He liked his ladies. His dark, fragile…beautiful ladies. He'd learned to appreciate them.

The councilman had just run into him in that darkness. The guy had been in his way, prey that he couldn't tolerate. A few thrusts of his knife, and Laxton Crenshaw hadn't been a problem, not any longer.

That just left me…and Ivy.

Such a wonderful surprise, to have her searching for him in the dark.

And she'd fought. He'd liked that. He never wanted his victims to just submit. Where was the fun there? He couldn't prove his dominance if they just waited for his knife.

I gave Ivy a choice. Because he always gave his ladies a choice. That was *his* rule. He could be good or he could be bad.

Ivy would determine her own fate.

So for now, he'd watch. He'd wait. And when the time was right...

Ivy, you will be mine. This time, he would get to keep the woman he wanted.

She would be his perfect prey.

Until death.

***

The ambulance's siren screeched in the night as it flew away from the scene. Ivy stood on the steps of the convention center, her gaze on that fleeing vehicle. Laxton had still been alive when he was loaded into the back of the ambulance. Would he survive until he reached the nearest hospital? She didn't know.

"What in the hell..." Bennett murmured beside her, "happened in that corridor?"

She shivered. Her arms were bare, the only covering they had was blood. Laxton's blood. Her dress was sleeveless and made for a ballroom, not the night. Wind blew against her, an icy touch that made her chill bumps all the worse.

"He was there," Ivy said. Her voice sounded hollow to her own ears. She wasn't supposed to sound that way. She wasn't supposed to be so afraid. Her grandfather wouldn't have been afraid.

He never would have let the killer get away.

"I ran into the killer in that hallway." Literally. "He'd...he'd already stabbed the councilman by then."

His hands closed around her shoulders and Bennett turned her to face him. "Describe him. Every detail."

"He still had on his mask and his tux. It was dark in there, and when he grabbed me, I dropped my phone so I couldn't even use that light." She'd have to go back for her phone. Later. When the area wasn't a crime scene.

"He...grabbed you?" There was a barely banked fury in his voice.

Ivy swallowed the lump in her throat. "He was wearing gloves," she recalled. Probably those fancy white gloves that so many guys wore to the balls. "I can remember what those gloves felt like when he wrapped his hands around my throat."

"He is a fucking dead man."

No, he wasn't. He was a man who'd gotten away. She struggled to recall more from that terrible scene and said, "His hair was dark. I saw it, before my phone broke. So dark it was almost black." Her chill was getting worse.

I'm going to learn your secrets. Your desires. I'm going to give you everything that you ever wanted.

"Ivy!"

Her head snapped up at the call and she saw her brother. Hugh was rushing toward her, pulling Shelly in his wake. Cameron was right at his side. Cameron had lost his mask and she could read the worry on his face.

Bennett backed away.

"He should've had blood on him," Ivy whispered. Her hand lifted and she rubbed her temple. "When he stabbed the councilman…he should have gotten blood on his tux." She stared at Bennett. "Why didn't anyone notice the blood?"

"Because it was damn chaos," Bennett gritted out. "Ivy—"

Hugh pulled her into his arms before Bennett could finish. She could feel the tremble that shook her brother. "Ivy, I was scared as hell." He squeezed her tighter. "I couldn't find you. I couldn't get to you." His tremble turned into a hard shudder. "What would I have done without you?"

"It's all right," she whispered. "I'm okay." Hugh always held his feelings so close to the vest, but when it came to her, she knew all bets were off. After their father had died, Hugh had clung even tighter to her. Become even *more* protective.

Cameron pushed Hugh back and started to give her a big hug—"Uh, Ivy." Cameron stopped his hugging attempt. "Is that blood?" His voice dropped. "A whole *lot* of blood?"

Bennett positioned himself between her and the others as he wrapped his arm around Ivy's shoulders. "She's coming with me. I'll make sure she's checked out and then I'll get her statement."

Her statement. Right. Only she didn't have a whole lot to state.

I can be good to you. Or, Ivy, my dear…I can be very, very bad…

"She's my sister," Hugh snapped. "I can take care of her, I can—"

"Hugh." Ivy's voice was soft. She knew how to handle her brother. Always had.

He blinked at her. She could see the worry and fear in his gaze. "I couldn't get to you," he said again.

Her head inclined toward him. "I'm okay." She kept her voice soft. "I-I saw the killer again."

Cameron swore.

Shelly backed up a step.

"He stabbed the councilman," Ivy said. She glanced down at her dress. "It's his blood, not mine."

Hugh started to pace. He did that when he was angry or afraid. Right then, she knew he was both. "The killer? Shit, when you told us about him in the limo, I didn't think you'd actually find him! I didn't think—"

"I think he found me. He knew my name, and he-he said things…" Things she didn't want to say, not with the crowd around them. Not with the familiar figures of reporters close by.

Bennett's hold tightened on Ivy's shoulders. "She's coming with me," he said again, only his voice was harder now. Almost daring someone to argue.

No one did.

Ivy just wanted to get out of there. She wanted to get the blood off. She wanted to forget the killer's voice.

I can be good to you.

So much for being some hotshot PI. She was shaking, nearly breaking apart on the inside.

"You sure you're okay?" Cameron asked her.

Cameron. He was a good guy, a good friend. Once, he'd tried to get them to be more, but it hadn't worked. *Because I'd still been hung up on Bennett.* Bennett had been her problem for a long time. It would have been nice if she could have wanted Cameron the way she wanted Bennett. Easier.

But life wasn't always easy.

"I'm okay," she promised him. "Don't worry about me. I'll call you tomorrow."

Then she let Bennett lead her away from them. As they walked through the crowd and Ivy heard the whispers around her, she couldn't help but wonder...

Was the killer close?

Was he watching her even now?

Had he taken off his mask? Blended in with everyone else?

Was he smiling as he followed her?

I can be good to you...

She hated having his voice in her head.

CHAPTER FOUR

It was close to dawn by the time Bennett parked his car near Ivy's house. He sat there a moment, with his hands on the steering wheel as he tried to figure out what the hell he should say to her.

Her gown had been collected as evidence. She'd been given a t-shirt—one that was way too big—and a pair of jogging pants that a female officer happened to have in her locker at the police station. Borrowed sneakers completed her outfit.

The damn thing was...Ivy was just as beautiful in those over-sized clothes as she'd been in that gorgeous gown. To him, Ivy was always gorgeous. No other woman had ever quite compared to her.

It sucks knowing you made the biggest mistake of your life when you were a nineteen year old kid. How many times had he wanted to go back and change the past? How many times had he thought of Ivy?

"Thanks for the lift home." She reached for her door handle, and the movement finally

jostled Bennett out of his stupor. He hurried out
of the car and raced around to her side. His aunt
had always instilled southern-boy manners in
him...and lesson one had been...

Always, always open the door for a lady.

He yanked open Ivy's door. "I'm coming in
the house."

She rose, quirked a brow and said, "Are you
now?"

Why was he always stumbling over his
words when it came to Ivy? Coming off too
pompous. And way too much like a jerk. He
cleared his throat and tried again. "I want to
make sure the house is safe. You said he knew
your name. It's not a big leap from knowing
your name to finding out where you live."

Her gaze turned to the house. "No," she
sounded sad now and he hated that. "It's not."

He shadowed her steps as she headed
toward her house. The place was huge, towering
above them and seeming to stretch toward the
sky. "You live here by yourself?"

And, yeah, there'd been an edge to his
words.

She paused on the porch and glanced at him.
"It's really been one hell of a night."

He figured that was an understatement.

"I'm tired, I'm pretty scared, and I can still
feel the guy touching me."

His hands fisted.

"So I'm going to save us both some time," Ivy told him as she turned to fully face him. "I'm not going to play any games."

He hated games.

"I live here alone. I'm not involved with anyone. I'm not sleeping with anyone—"

"Cameron—"

She rolled her eyes. "I'm not sleeping with Cameron."

"But you were."

Silence.

Jealousy burned in his gut.

"How do you know about that?" Ivy's voice was far too soft.

"Because maybe I came back to town one day, desperate to see you. And maybe—maybe I learned I'd come home too late. You were already in bed with him."

She sucked in a sharp breath. "I slept with Cameron once. And *I* don't have to apologize for that. We weren't together. You were long gone. I was alone—with the wreck of my life that had been left behind."

"Shit, Ivy, I'm sorry." And he was. "You don't have to tell me—"

"I didn't want him, not the way I wanted you."

His heart stopped.

"Cameron was my friend, and I didn't want to screw that up. I needed my friends then. Needed them badly. But I tried again, Bennett.

Know that. I wanted to find someone else who'd make me feel the way you did — who'd make me feel even better."

He'd deal with the jealousy. He'd *deal*. But he wouldn't screw this up again.

"You know what really sucks?" Ivy whispered.

Not having you. That was what sucked for him.

"I couldn't find anyone."

He took a step back. Oh, hell…was she saying…did he still have a chance? "Ivy…"

"Are you going to search my house or are you going to keep torturing me?"

He wanted to touch her. He wanted to take away every bit of pain she'd ever felt. His life had changed — dramatically — in the last year. He'd gotten his priorities in order. He'd come back to Mobile because priority one was Ivy. He'd just needed a way to approach her.

I didn't think a murder would be the path that brought us back together. "No torture," he promised, his voice rough.

She turned from him and reached for the door handle. Before she could unlock the door, he caught her hand. His body moved in, and he caged her between him and that door.

"I never stay with a lover long," he whispered, bending close to her ear. "Because the other women aren't you." That was *his* problem. One that tormented him. You weren't supposed to find a perfect lover when you were barely a man, but he had. He'd found Ivy, and after her...

No one else had ever compared. No one could. Without her, he'd learned too late...he was lost.

She didn't move, but she did say, "I thought you'd come to me, once you were back in town."

He had, the very day that he'd returned to Mobile. He'd come to this damn house. He'd stayed across the street. He'd stared up at her lighted windows. He'd seen her silhouette.

I was like some stalker. And he'd been afraid. Afraid to walk up to that door and knock. Afraid she'd send his ass away.

Then he'd seen her being pushed toward the back of a patrol car...

Causing trouble again? Those had been his words, and they'd nearly stuck in his throat. He'd wanted to say...*Ivy, dear God, I missed you.*

"If you really wanted me," Ivy said. "You should have told me."

"I'm not good for you. We both know that." He wanted to kiss the curve of her neck. Or maybe bite the shell of her ear. She'd always liked that, before.

"I don't remember asking you to stay away." Her voice was husky. "I never asked that. Not then, and not now."

She was about to gut him. "It's a dangerous path you're taking. I walked away once. You expect me to do it again?"

Ivy turned then, her body brushing against his. "I don't expect anything of you, Bennett. That's the beauty of the situation these days. I can go into a relationship with my eyes wide open. I can say no strings, and I can mean it."

There'd always been strings between them. Strings that connected them, no matter how far away they were.

Didn't I come back, just for her?

He could have gone to any other town. He'd gotten better offers, much higher pay. But…

She was here.

"Now…why don't you come inside?"

Every muscle in his body tensed.

"And do a thorough check of the place," she continued quickly, "because — and don't freak out — I don't have an alarm set up, and I'd really feel better if we both went in together."

No alarm? Oh, the hell, *no.*

He backed up a step and waited for her to head inside. The door creaked as she opened it. When they entered the cavernous house, Ivy quickly flipped the light switch, flooding the foyer with illumination.

"I've been fixing the place up." Ivy waved her hand to the walls as Bennett locked the door. "Fresh paint. New flooring. Even a new banister on the stairs. It's a slow process, but, one day, this place is going to be amazing again."

"Amazing," Bennett said, but his gaze was on Ivy.

She gave him a faint smile. "Team work, right?" Her voice sharpened. "Let's get this search done."

And they did. They went through the whole house, and what Bennett saw truly pissed him off. *Too many places to hide.* Too many ways to get inside. Too many unsecured windows. "You need an alarm. *Now.*"

"Right. It's already on my to-do list," she said as they paused in front of her bedroom. They were on the second floor. Half of that floor had been remodeled, half was shut down, empty. "I didn't expect a killer to be coming after me. I didn't expect—" She broke off as her gaze slid from his. "I should shower. I-I think I may still have blood on me."

Bennett crossed his arms over his chest. "I know you didn't tell me everything at the station."

She was looking down at her hands. There was no blood on them. She'd scrubbed them, again and again, while he watched her at the station.

"Ivy."

Her head lifted. "I told you all that I remembered about the guy's description."

That part he believed. "Did you tell me everything he said?" He knew his witnesses—and his victims. He could tell when they were holding back, and every instinct he possessed screamed that Ivy was keeping secrets.

She wet her lips. "He was just trying to scare me." She laughed then, a bitter sound that wasn't at all what he'd associate with Ivy. "I'm a PI. I'm not supposed to be scared, I'm not—"

"Everyone gets scared sometimes."

Her gaze held his. "Even you, Bennett?"

He nodded and for just an instant, his last case with the Bureau flashed before his eyes. Pain. Blood. Hell.

No escape.

He'd stared at death and he'd seen...

Ivy.

"Bennett?"

"If you're human, you get scared," he told her flatly. "That's normal. No matter who the hell you are."

Her breath expelled in a fast rush. "I really need that shower." A thread of desperation laced through her words. "I can feel the blood and...*him.*"

Bennett couldn't wait to catch that bastard and throw him in a cell. "He's not going to hurt you," he said as he took a step closer to Ivy.

She gave a quick nod. "I'll show you out. I—"

"I'll wait until you're done with that shower. Then you *are* going to tell me everything." This time, there would be no secrets between them. It was the secrets that had destroyed them before.

Bennett wasn't about to repeat the mistakes from his past.

***

Ivy scrubbed her skin until it ached. She scrubbed and scrubbed, but she could have sworn the blood was still on her.

And that I can still feel his touch.

But the water in the shower turned icy, and she knew she had to leave and face Bennett again. She dressed quickly, tossing on some old sweats and a very faded college sweatshirt. Her wet hair slid around her face, curling slightly, and she padded, barefoot, down her stairs.

Bennett was waiting in what her grandfather would have called the parlor. A fancy word that had always made her smile when she was younger, even though she just thought of that place as a den now.

Bennett turned when she approached, surprising her because Ivy had thought that she'd been moving pretty silently. His gaze swept from the top of her wet head down to her toes — toes that were currently painted with a bright blue polish. His lips curled, just a bit when he gazed at her toes.

His smile made her remember the past — their past. Did he know that she'd loved him back then? Probably not. She hadn't told him. Sometimes she'd wondered…if he'd known how she felt, would that have changed anything?

The silence was stretching between them, and a heavy tension coiled in the air. Ivy cleared her throat and hurried past him. She sat down on her overstuffed couch and tucked her legs under her. "The killer said that he saw me. That I saw him, and he saw me."

Bennett strode toward her. He didn't sit, just stood there, towering over her. Making her feel too nervous and aware of him.

"You told me that part at the station," he said.

Yes, she had.

"You told me…" Bennett's voice was a deep rumble. "That he knew your name. That he said he knew your brother. When you first found the councilman, you thought that *was* Hugh's body."

"Yes." When would the memory of that terror end? But beneath the fear, anger simmered. That man—that bastard in the dark— he'd *wanted* her to think that Hugh was hurt or dead. He'd been playing with her, tormenting her.

And I think the torment is just beginning.

Her hands rose and she touched her throat. "I don't think he expected me to fight back." Had he thought she'd be too afraid? No, not happening. Her grandfather had taught her better than that. *Never let fear control you. Use it, Ivy. Use it and let it make you stronger.* His words whispered through her head.

"He told me I would be fun," she glanced at Bennett. As she said those words, his jaw hardened. "He told me," Ivy continued, "that he could be 'good' to me."

Bennett swore.

"Or that he could be 'bad'." Ivy paused a moment, considering that. "I'll just assume the 'bad' is when he takes out his knife and starts carving into people."

Bennett started pacing. "This isn't a damn game, Ivy!"

"I know. I told him the same thing."

He whirled to face her.

"I think I'm his next target."

His eyes changed then. So did his face. All emotion just bled away.

"He said…" *Finish it.* She just hadn't been able to reveal all of this down at the station, not with all those eyes on her. Strangers. Staring, judging? "He told me that he was going to give me…um, everything I wanted. That he'd learn my secrets. My d-desires."

Bennett stalked toward her. Her head tipped back as she looked up at him.

"The hell he will." Then he bent over her. His hand curled around her chin, as his face came intimately close to her. "This isn't happening to you."

Her breath seemed to burn her lungs. "What aren't you telling me?"

His green eyes glittered.

"Bennett…"

"He attacked two people within a twenty-four hour period, Ivy. What does that *tell* you?"

"He's dangerous." Serious understatement. "I thought…with the woman…maybe it was a crime of passion." A love that had ended in horror. "And the councilman, in the dark, in that tunnel, maybe—"

"This guy is very good at killing. Too good. *No one* reported seeing a man leave either scene with blood on his clothes." He released her chin, but didn't move back. "That means the guy knows how to use his weapon. He understands exactly how to sink a knife into his victim's skin so that the blood spatter doesn't so much as touch him."

She swallowed. "You…you think he's done this before."

"Hell, yes, I do. Because a killer doesn't show this much confidence on a new attack. A new hunter wouldn't come to you, he wouldn't make threats, and he wouldn't *target* you that way." He shook his head. "It's all wrong. If that woman had been his first kill, he would panic, thinking the police were involved. He wouldn't seek you out and tell you what he had planned next. That's a cocky move. Deliberate." He hesitated, then said, "Taunting."

She stood and he moved back, just a bit. His gaze was so intense. She couldn't look away. "You're telling me—what? That you think this guy is some kind of-of serial killer or something?"

"I don't know *what* kind of killer he is, not yet. All I know is that he's dangerous, and every single sign is pointing to him being focused on you."

The last twenty-four hours of her life hadn't been such winners. "I wanted to find him at that ball. I wanted to stop him."

"We are going to stop him," Bennett said. "Count on it."

They were so close. Adrenaline still spiked her blood. She'd been afraid. She'd been furious. And now...

"This isn't a case where you're just trying to uncover some rich businessman's secret affairs, Ivy. This isn't about finding out who stole an antique watch or tracking down a runaway teenager through your PI office..."

Her chin notched up. "If you're saying—"

"I'm saying, yes, I know you handle plenty of PI cases, but this is different. This is life and death, and I am *not* going to stand by while you get hurt."

No standing by. She got that. Her hands rose and pressed to his chest. She felt him stiffen beneath her touch.

"Ivy..."

"I don't want you to stand by." She didn't intend to just play the role of the victim, either. "We're going to be partners."

"The hell we are!"

"We *are* going to be partners," she said again. "Because if he is hunting me, then I want you at my side."

His gaze searched hers. "You always think you can control everyone around you."

No, she didn't think that.

"Men jump to do your bidding, and you just take that shit for granted."

"I don't remember you ever jumping." Quite the opposite. She remembered him leaving.

"Things aren't going to keep working that way. I'm not going to risk you."

I'm not yours to risk. She didn't say those words, not yet. But they still seemed to hang in the air between them. He didn't understand her. Maybe he never had. Did he think she was just playing at the PI business? No, things were different now. Everything was different.

The fact that she was intimately involved in this murder just made her all the more determined to act — and to prove herself.

Chasing cheating husbands, my ass.

"Thanks for seeing me home, *Detective*," she pulled away from him and marched back to the foyer. "I'm quite safe now. So you've done your due diligence."

His steps were slower as he followed her. "I can stay, if you want."

She looked back at him. "You think he's going to come for me again, this soon?"

"I didn't think he'd drive his knife into the councilman's chest, but he did."

Her shoulders straightened. "I'll be fine." She kept a gun under her bed. And that night, she'd be making sure it was loaded.

A furrow appeared between Bennett's brows.

"Goodbye, Bennett," she told him firmly.

He didn't move. "I want to stay."

"Excuse me?"

"It's...hell, it's important, Ivy. I need to know you're safe." His hands were clenched at his sides. "Until I get a better handle on this case, until I can figure out what the fuck is going on...I need this. I need to be close to you."

He had no idea how much his words hurt. Because those were words she'd wished to hear long ago. Not the whole "what the fuck is going on" part but...

I need to be close to you.

"You can stay upstairs. There's a guest room down the hallway that you can use." Her voice was grudging and she sighed. "Of course, you know my neighbors will see your car. Everyone will say we're sleeping together." *Again.*

He stared at her. "I thought you never cared what people said."

"I don't." She turned and headed for the stairs. "Just thought you should know..."

He snagged her hand. "Are we going to talk about it?"

She looked at his hand. So much tanner than her own. So much bigger. Stronger. "You mean the kiss?" She gave a faint laugh. "It was so fast, I hardly think that—"

"Actually, I meant our past, but, yeah, if you want to talk about the kiss, let's do it."

Crap. She'd walked straight into that one.

"Want to know why I kissed you?"

Get out of here. Right now. That warning was flashing in her head and she kept a faint smile on her face as she looked up at him. "I already know why."

"You do?"

"Because you still want me."

His eyes narrowed.

"Want to know why I kissed you back?" Ivy asked him as she pulled away and then headed up the stairs.

"Why." A demand, not a question.

She stilled on the fifth step. Her hand tightened around the banister. "Because I never *stopped* wanting you."

"Ivy…"

She kept going up the stairs. "Enjoy the guest room." Because she might want him, she might need him, but she wasn't crossing that line. Not yet.

Not when I'm already close to breaking apart on the inside.

He didn't understand just what her life had become. She wasn't about playing things safe. Being the *good* DuLane, not anymore.

And she wasn't ready to share her dark secrets with him, not yet.

***

"I see you," he whispered as he stared up at the house. Ivy was in that house. Ivy and the detective.

Were they lovers? Screwing on the stairs? On the floor? In Ivy's bed?

That wouldn't do. *He'd* picked her. She was his now, for as long as he wanted.

And he kept his prey until the last breath.

The detective would require some research, just as Ivy would. He liked to study his prey. Learn their strengths and weaknesses.

The councilman — he'd been different. *The fool got in my way.* But it was for the best. He couldn't afford any loose ends. Too much was at stake.

He'd learned that Laxton hadn't made it to the hospital alive, despite Ivy's valiant efforts.

How would she react to that news? Would lovely Ivy blame herself? Would she cry?

He isn't worth your tears. Save them all for me.

He turned away from Ivy's house. He wouldn't be visiting her, not yet. There was more to learn first. More arrangements to make.

Soon enough, Ivy would have her turn.

I'll learn those secrets, and those desires. In the end, she would beg for him.

His prey always did.

CHAPTER FIVE

Ivy didn't usually hang out in morgues. They were creepy, seriously creepy. They smelled bad. They were cold. And they made her stomach knot.

"Are you okay?"

Ivy sucked in a quick breath and tried really hard not to gag. She so did not have this calm, in-command attitude down. Bennett ruled that kind of attitude. Damn him.

"Ivy, you look like you're about to faint," the ME said. He was an older guy, balding, with warm coffee skin and sympathetic brown eyes.

Beside him, Bennett grunted. He was *not* so sympathetic. "She shouldn't even be here. She can wait in the hallway and—"

"Thanks for letting me come in, Dr. Battiste," Ivy said quickly. "I appreciate it."

Bennett had looked way less-than-thrilled when she'd trailed him to the morgue. His expression had darkened even more when it became obvious that she and Harvey Battiste knew each other. She'd actually known Harvey since she was about three, when she'd been sneaking off with Harvey and her grandfather on their fishing trips.

Harvey frowned at her, but he didn't argue. Instead, he turned toward his exam table and motioned toward the body on display. "Our victim is twenty-five-year-old Evette Summers. Her fingerprints turned up in the system, so ID'ing her was easy." He exhaled. "She was stabbed four times, and it appears when the blade was plunging into her, the killer…twisted the weapon, seeking maximum damage."

Ivy's nails bit into her palms.

"There weren't defensive wounds on the victim." Harvey rubbed his chin. "Based on the angle of entry, I doubt our victim *could* fight back after the first drive of that knife into her."

"And she didn't even realize the attack was coming," Ivy said.

Harvey blinked.

Ivy moved, positioning her body in front of Bennett's as she remembered that terrible scene. "They were like this when I first saw them." She pushed her back against Bennett. She took his left arm, wrapped it around her body, and then with his right… "A lover's pose. She probably thought she was totally safe, until the blade went into her the first time."

Bennett's hold tightened on Ivy.

"Then it was too late," she said sadly. "All she had time to do was scream for help." Help that Ivy hadn't given to her.

Harvey nodded. "I *have* started an exam on Councilman Crenshaw."

Ivy flinched and moved away from Bennett. She'd heard that the councilman hadn't survived long enough to reach the hospital.

"He had defensive wounds. And his stab wounds were centered close to his heart. A chest attack."

"Shouldn't there have been spatter from that kind of attack?" Bennett demanded.

Ivy stared down at the woman on that exam table. She was only a year younger than Ivy. Their hair was the same. Their bone structure even similar...

"There should have been," Harvey agreed, "but you said your perp had on a tux, right? Maybe when he was leaving, he just ditched his jacket. The blood could have been on it, and nothing else he wore."

"Maybe that jacket is still at the convention center," Bennett mused. "I'll get the crime scene team to search again. We can't afford to miss something like that."

No, they couldn't.

Ivy inched closer to the exam table.

"Have there been more?" Bennett asked quietly.

Ivy's gaze cut to him.

"Any other victims brought in like her?" Bennett pressed. "With stab wounds like hers? Knives are intimate weapons. The weapons that killers use when they like to get up close and feel their victims die. A power rush."

Okay…He was creeping her out a bit. Sounding a bit too much like he understood the killer.

Harvey rubbed his chin, seeming to think about it. "I'll have to pull my records, but I seem to recall a Jane Doe with similar wounds who was discovered down here, right about Mardi Gras…about two years ago."

Two years.

"And there might have been one more." Harvey headed toward the exam table. He stared down at the woman — at Evette — but Ivy felt as if he weren't actually seeing her. "A younger victim, about four years ago. Nineteen years old, twenty? She was stabbed, too, but actually…she was killed in New Orleans. A colleague told me about her. Her story stuck with me because…" Now his attention shifted back to Bennett. "Because she was found during Mardi Gras, too. And I remember he said finding her killer was going to be damn near impossible because the Big Easy goes mad during the Mardi Gras party."

Three potential victims. Four, counting the councilman. Ivy knew this was big. Scary big.

"I want to see all of those case files," Bennett instructed. "Right away. Give me what you've got on the local victims, and I'd really appreciate you putting in a call to your friend in New Orleans, too."

Harvey nodded. "Of course."

I need to see those files, too. But she couldn't very well say that, not with Bennett standing there and glowering.

"Thanks for your time," she told the doctor even as she made a mental note to call him later. Harvey would give her the info she needed. After all, he was practically family.

Bennett took her elbow and rather hurriedly escorted her from the ME's office. As soon as they were in the hallway and that door closed behind them...

"What in the hell!" Bennett exclaimed. "You aren't supposed to be here!"

She squinted up at him. "Where should I be?"

"Getting a security system installed!" He threw up his hands.

"Oh, yes, Hugh is supervising that for me. No worries." She gave him a bright smile. "A little bird told me about your meeting with the ME, and I figured it was important for me to attend."

"Important?" The word seemed strangled.

"Since we're partners and all —"

"We are *not* partners!"

She sighed. "Fine. We're two independent investigators who happen to be working the same case."

Jaw locked, he gritted out, "I'm the homicide detective in charge and *you* are a witness and a potential victim. You aren't investigating the case."

"Um, I kind of…am, investigating, that is."

His lips parted, but he didn't speak. Maybe he couldn't. Ivy would consider that a win for her. "There's no point fighting this," Ivy told him bluntly. "I've got more connections in this town than you can count. I'll get the info that I need and we can either share things, or, well, I can get ahead of you."

His eyes squeezed closed. She felt as if he did that a lot.

"Are we going back to the convention center now?" Ivy asked him. "Because I think we need to be there when the crime scene techs sweep again for that jacket. They won't have a whole lot of time, you know. Another ball is scheduled to occur there tonight, and there's *no way* the mayor will let that place stay a crime scene. Too much rides on Mardi Gras, and you know it."

His eyes cracked open. "I'm going to the convention center."

Uh…

"*You* are staying away from my case. You're a civilian."

Why did he make that word sound like a curse?

"It's too dangerous for you to get involved in this case." Then his hands closed around her shoulders. His voice softened. "Don't you see that I'm just trying to protect you?"

And don't you see that I'm trying to help the victim?

Their gazes held.

"Same old Ivy," he finally muttered. "You think your family's money can buy your way just about any place, don't you?"

His words hurt. He didn't know what she'd done — he didn't know anything about her. "Same old Bennett," she whispered back, aching for them both. "Seeing only what you want to see. And missing out on something great right in front of you." She pulled away from him. "Good luck with your investigation." Then she headed down the hallway.

She didn't look back.

***

"I couldn't help but overhear…"

Bennett glanced over his shoulder as the door to the ME's office opened. Dr. Battiste lifted his brow. "Well, I overheard because I was listening."

What the hell?

"I don't like the way you were talking to Ivy."

He was starting to think that everyone around him was insane. "This case isn't some walk in the park." No, if his gut was right...then they might just be looking at a serial killer.

Not the fuck again. He'd barely escaped the last serial he'd faced, and he had the scars to prove it. The bastard had nearly gutted him, and Bennett had watched as his partner died right in front of him.

And Ivy thinks I'll let her partner with me on this case? Hell, no. The last thing he ever wanted was her put at risk.

"Ivy knows how to handle the dark side of life," Dr. Battiste said.

She did? Since when? His head cocked as he studied the doctor. "You're the little bird."

"Can't say I've been called that before..."

"You told Ivy that I was coming in today, didn't you?"

Dr. Battiste shrugged.

"Why would you do that? She doesn't need to be involved."

"If he's hunting her, then she needs to know everything about this case." Dr. Battiste's voice was flat.

He was missing something. Something big.

Dr. Battiste smiled at him. "Ivy and I meet for lunch on Saturdays. Every Saturday. Since her grandfather passed, well, someone needed to fill that void for her. I'm the one who taught that girl how to bait her first fishing hook, and I'm the one who watched her cry when she learned that the fish die once they're reeled in...Ivy doesn't like to kill things, you see. She learned real quick how to catch and release…"

He hadn't realized how close those two were. Actually, he hadn't known they were close at all.

"You really think all she and her grandfather did was take fluff cases?"

He didn't —

"I didn't know you were that piss poor of a cop." Dr. Battiste walked past him. "My mistake. Why don't you try doing a little research on the Sebastian Jones murder? Go see what you turn up, *Detective Morgan*."

Bennett watched him go, frowning now.

And wondering if he knew Ivy at all.

***

"Why in the hell do you want to do this to yourself?"

Ivy glanced up at Hugh's question. They were in her den, no, the *parlor,* and she'd just pulled up a search engine on her computer. Dr. Battiste had emailed her the names of the other potential victims, and she wanted to see what she could find on them. "This?" she asked carefully.

He sighed and shook his head. His hair was the same dark shade of her own, his eyes a deep brown. He was the older twin, by fifteen minutes. Older…and stronger. At least at birth.

He'd been six pounds. She'd been barely three.
She'd stayed in intensive care for weeks. Her
mother had told her that the doctors hadn't been
sure she'd survive.

She had.

"Why do you keep trying to atone for what
he did?"

Her shoulders stiffened. "I don't know what
you mean." She closed her laptop, not wanting
him to see her search. "Are the security installers
done?"

"Yeah, you're good to go. They're waiting to
show you how the system works."

She stood and hurried around her desk.

Hugh didn't move. "You think I don't feel
guilty, too?"

"This isn't about our guilt."

"Of course, it is. You're trying to save the
world because you think it can make up for
what he did. But you can't save everyone, Ivy.
And, after last night, I think we just need to
focus on saving *you*."

She put her hand on his arm. "I don't need
saving."

"Bullshit."

"Hugh…"

"I know about the cases you've taken. Did
you even get paid for them?"

No, not all but—

"You've been walking a dangerous line for years, and it's got to stop. If it doesn't, you're going to get hurt."

Her breath heaved out. "I didn't go looking for this case, all right? I saw that woman die. I just wanted to help her."

Hugh was so much taller than she was. "Who will help you, though, Ivy? If you're caught alone in the dark again with that SOB, who will be there for you?"

She didn't have an answer for him. Bennett wasn't going to be her partner, and for all of her other cases, well, she'd been working them on her own.

"The danger is too much. Hell, I don't like this shit. Not one bit." His breath rushed out. "Maybe I should move in and stay for a while. Until the PD catches this guy. You don't need to be alone—"

"I wasn't alone after the attack at the convention center. Bennett was here."

Hugh's face hardened. "He's no good for you, Ivy. How many times do I have to tell you that?"

"You can tell me a thousand times, but it won't matter." She didn't pull her punches with Hugh. "Bennett and I aren't done." Even though he'd royally pissed her off at the ME's office. "You need to accept that."

"So is he going to be here tonight, is he going to be here with you, every night, until that killer is behind bars?"

"I don't know what he plans." She stepped around him. "All I know is that I have to see some men about an alarm…"

***

Hugh watched his sister walk away. Ivy didn't get it. She couldn't fix the world, even though he knew that was *exactly* what she'd been trying to do for far too long.

He'd always known that Ivy was the good twin. The one who looked out at the world and hoped.

While he…

I know exactly what I am. And it's not good.

If he found the jerk who'd terrorized his sister in that hallway last night, the guy wasn't going to make it to the inside of a jail cell. No one hurt his family and gets away scot-free.

No one.

It was a lesson that he thought Bennett Morgan had learned years ago.

***

"You're going back with him. Aren't you?"

Ivy glanced over at Cameron. He'd arrived at her house just as the security installers had left. And since then, he'd been pacing around like a caged tiger, the energy seeming to roll off him.

"Cameron…"

"Bennett Morgan is no good for you."

So she kept being told. Even though she didn't remember asking what anyone else thought of Bennett.

Cameron moved to stand in front of her bay window. "I would have given you anything you wanted. You should have stayed with me."

Oh, no. *No, no, no.* They couldn't be back to this. Ivy jumped to her feet and hurried toward him. Then…then she couldn't touch him. Fear held her back. *I don't want to hurt him.* "Cameron, you know I love you."

He looked back at her. His lips had twisted. "Like a friend."

"No, more than that. Like family. You matter to me, so much."

His gaze lowered.

"I'm not *in* love with you, Cameron, and you're not in love with me." She knew that with certainty. The guy had a new flavor of the week always waiting in the wings. "I think we heard too many people tell us that we *should* be together when we were younger, but we weren't right that way. We didn't fit."

"Not the way you fit with Bennett."

Bennett infuriated her. He drove her to the edge and…

Yes, when she was with him, she still felt like she fit.

The connection between her and Bennett had been so strong — from the very beginning — and maybe it had even scared her a little. *Am I supposed to give so much of myself to him?*

She had. Too late, she'd realized that she'd given Bennett everything.

"I don't want to see you get hurt." Now Cameron sounded grim. "But that's going to happen, Ivy. You *will* be hurt."

"Things are different."

"Yes, they are." He marched around her and picked up his coat. "I think I'll get out of town for a bit. Maybe spend some time at the beach house."

She hurried after him. "Cameron…" She'd been clear with him, for years, and for this to come back up now…

He looked back at her. "I think it's time I put that particular dream to bed. I saw the way you looked at him. And I saw the way he looked back at you. The past isn't over."

Then he was striding toward the door. She followed him out onto the porch and watched as he jumped into his SUV and drove away. Ivy didn't immediately go back inside. She stood there, aching, so sad that she'd caused Cameron pain.

Things would have been easier, if she had been able to lose herself with him. But that hadn't happened. And she'd known it wouldn't be right to use him.

He deserved more.

So do I.

She could hear the sound of the parade, drifting in the air. It was Saturday night — more floats would be filling the streets, and the boom of drum beats echoed around her. That sound used to soothe her, but it didn't anymore. She tensed, her heart raced faster. Her arms wrapped around her stomach as she listened to those sounds. The bands were marching. The crowd cheering.

Was the killer out there again? Hiding in that crowd. Watching everyone?

A car turned down her street. She tensed for a moment, but then recognized the vehicle. Ivy didn't move from her positon as Bennett parked near the curb. He exited quickly, and hurried toward her.

He looked big. Strong. Dangerous. Typical Bennett.

The exact opposite of Cameron. In so many ways.

She'd been doing some digging on him since their last little meeting. Digging on him and the other potential victims. Nothing she'd learned had been particularly reassuring.

In fact, it had been quite the opposite.

He stopped at the foot of her porch and stared up at her. "Your new alarm system won't do you much good if you're outside."

"And staying locked away for the rest of my life won't do me a whole lot of *good* either."

His lips hitched into a half-smile. "Touché."

She didn't smile back. "Is there a reason for this little visit?"

"Yeah, I wanted to check on you."

She shook her head. "I don't have to be watched twenty-four hours a day."

He put his foot on the bottom step. "Maybe you shouldn't be too sure about that."

She tried to read his expression. The light from her porch spilled onto him. "What did you learn?"

"I talked with Evette's family. They said she'd hooked up with a man she called Robert Adderly — they met about a week ago at a ball. Evette seemed to fall hard for the guy, and she told her mother he was perfect. Smart, handsome, rich."

Ivy waited.

"Only the mother — and none of Evette's friends — actually met Robert. And when I tried to do a search on the guy, I couldn't find him. At least, not a guy matching that description. I did find one Robert Adderly living in Mobile, but he's an eighty-eight year old gentlemen currently residing in a nursing facility."

"So you think that her lover gave her a false name."

"I think he fed her plenty of lies. I think he got close to her, he enjoyed her, used her, and when he was done…"

No defensive wounds.

"She never even had a chance to fight," Bennett said.

Ivy rubbed her arms. "And the others that Dr. Battiste mentioned? Did they have mystery men in their lives, too?" She already knew this part, though.

"You tell me," he invited.

Uh, oh…

"Because Fiona Hargrave — she was the woman found in Mobile about two years ago — her mother said that she talked with an investigator today. A woman who wanted to know about the men in Fiona's life."

Ivy shrugged. "Guilty."

He climbed another step. They were on eye level now. "You know that Fiona also had a lover, one that her family never met. A man who called himself William Walker."

She nodded.

"The victim in New Orleans had a lover, too. Her family didn't meet him."

There was no missing that pattern.

"No lover showed for any of the funerals," Bennett added. "The guy just vanished when the women turned up dead."

"Of course, he vanished," she said, speaking softly, "he was done with them." *He'd already*

moved on to someone new...just like he did with me.
Evette's body had barely been cold, and he'd
already been tormenting Ivy. Only... "He didn't
try to seduce me."

"Good fucking thing," Bennett muttered.

She shook her head. "No, you don't
understand." And, yes, she *had* talked to the
families. She'd called them and told them that
she was a private investigator interested in
solving cold cases. They'd been hesitant at first,
but they'd answered her questions.

*And they'd been grateful...glad someone was
still looking for answers.* Because they'd felt as if
their daughters had been buried and forgotten
by the rest of the world.

"These women were all infatuated with the
men they knew." That had been clear in the
phone calls. "They told their families wonderful
things about the man." *If* it had been the same
man. "But he didn't try to charm me or trick me.
He came at me, showing me exactly what he
was. Not pretending anything else."

Why?

She hadn't seen his face. She wouldn't have
known if he'd walked up to her and flirted. Hell,
she *still* didn't know what he looked like.

"Something is different with me," Ivy said.
And that made her nervous.

"Maybe *you're* just different." Bennett gazed
at her. "You saw him kill. Maybe that makes you

different. Maybe you saw him for what he is, and maybe the bastard likes that."

A shiver swept over her. "Maybe."

It was good, being on eye level with him. Being so close to him. Their bodies were close, but not touching. The temptation to touch him was strong, but she didn't move.

"I like that coat," Bennett remarked.

Her lips parted and she glanced down. "Oh, sorry!" *His* coat. She'd put it on without really thinking about it before and she shouldered out of it.

"No." He put his hand on her shoulder. "Keep it. I've got more."

So did she.

He didn't pull his hand back.

"You know killers." Those weren't the words she'd meant to say. Were they?

His hand lifted and he brushed back the hair that had fallen over her cheek. "Yes." He seemed sad. "I do."

"Y-you worked Violent Crimes." She had a few federal connections — courtesy of her father — that she'd used to dig into his past.

Bennett gave a low whistle. "You have been busy today. I should have known you weren't just walking away to spend a lazy Saturday someplace."

She never spent lazy Saturdays anywhere. "How many killers did you take down?"

"Ivy…" Now a warning edge entered his voice.

She wasn't backing off. "Tell me about your last case." Because *that* was the one that mattered. The one that had changed everything for him. And, try as she might, that case had remained classified.

She had uncovered only the barest of facts. Bennett and his partner had been working a case, tracking a suspected serial killer. The suspect had been killed. Bennett's partner had been killed. And Bennett had spent a week in the hospital.

After he was released, he'd taken a month leave from the Bureau. Then, abruptly, he'd quit and headed back to Alabama.

He'd almost died, and I didn't even know it.

Strange…to think of how much his death would have hurt her, when they'd been apart for so long.

"You don't want to hear about that case."

"Actually, I do. I want to hear everything about you."

He eased down a step. "I have some photos at the station that I want you to come and take a look at. Pictures that were snapped by people at the ball. The press was filming the scene when everyone left, and it's possible we have our perp on camera."

Was that his way of saying he wasn't about to tell her about that last case or why he'd suddenly left the FBI? Did he think she was just going to drop it? No, she'd get her answers, sooner or later. She always did. "Let's go," Ivy said. It wasn't as if she had any other thrilling plans for the night. She could hear voices drifting to her — soon the parades would be in full force.

She didn't want to be alone that night. Better to go with Bennett and see those photos.

Better to be with him.

She locked her house. Set the new alarm. Then they walked together over to the street. Bennett opened the passenger door. She slid inside, and his rich, masculine scent seemed to follow her. He shut the passenger door behind her and walked around the vehicle. Her gaze darted down her street, one of those historic streets lined with oaks that were at least a hundred years old. Spanish moss hung from the oaks, drifting lightly in the breeze. The trees were gorgeous. She'd always loved them but...

But they sent dark shadows sweeping through the neighborhood. They provided so many hiding spaces.

Bennett closed his door. He slid into the seat and cranked the engine. Ivy eased out a low breath and straightened her shoulders. For an instant there, she'd almost been sure that someone *was* hiding in the shadows. Watching. Waiting.

Maybe she was just letting her imagination get the better of her.

As the car headed down the street, she couldn't help but glance back at the shadows.

Or maybe not.

***

Ivy had left...*with* that jerk detective. The man was proving to be an annoyance. He'd kept tabs on the detective that day. He knew Bennett Morgan was messing with the dead. He should leave the ladies to rest, and not go digging into their past.

Into my past.

He'd always been so careful with the kills. One in New Orleans, one in Mobile. Always planning them right when Mardi Gras was in full swing. The cities were packed then — hotels overflowing. It was so easy to vanish in those crowds. So easy to kill. And he'd learned that if he played things just right, the bodies weren't even found for days, or weeks after those parades and parties ended.

So perfect. So brilliant.

But...

Ivy saw me. For the first time, someone had watched while he killed. And he'd liked that. Liked it so fucking much to have her eyes on him while he drove his knife into a victim.

And everything that he learned about Ivy, every new secret that was revealed, told him just how truly perfect she was for him.

She looked like his victims. So beautiful. So breakable.

But...

But there's more to her. She's important, I know it.

He stared up at her house. More of Ivy's secrets were in that house. He wanted in there. He wanted to be waiting for her when the cop brought her back.

But Ivy had installed a new security system. He'd watched that installation. Even come up and talked with the security team when they'd been taking a break outside. He knew she'd gotten a good system, one that he might not be able to bypass.

His eyes narrowed.

But I want in.

And what he wanted, he got.

CHAPTER SIX

There were dozens of videos. And easily several thousand pictures. Ivy stared at them until she was sure her eyes burned, but she didn't see any sign of the killer. Or, if she did, she didn't realize it.

He had on a mask. It was dark. Dammit, the only thing I know about him is that his hair is dark and he's built like Bennett.

"No luck?"

She looked up at Bennett's voice. She was in his office, sitting at his desk, and he'd just appeared in the doorway. His voice hadn't been particularly hopeful, and she saw that his expression was grim.

"No, I'm sorry."

He nodded. "It was a long shot. There are so many exits from that convention center, and the place was total chaos."

"No bloody clothes were found?"

"Not by the crime team, and they went back again earlier, searching for it." He crossed the room and came to her side, standing over her as he looked down at the computer. "It's really the perfect place, if you think about it. All of those people, many of them already so drunk they can't stand...and even if they *aren't* drunk, then maybe they've had enough to be buzzing a bit. They won't remember what they saw. Throw in the masks and the darkness, and you have your total anonymity. If you wanted to commit a crime, if you wanted to hurt someone...do it right there. No one will know."

She shivered because his voice had turned so cold. "Is that what you think he's been doing? Killing in the crowds for what — the last few years?"

"It's what makes sense. A prime hunting ground."

Okay, that was creepy. But she didn't speak because she knew exactly what he was doing — profiling the killer. He'd probably done that before, when he'd been working Violent Crimes. She wanted to hear what else he had to say.

"His victims look alike," Ivy said as she craned her head to look up at him. *They look like me.*

"And that's why he's probably thrilled right now." His eyes glinted. "Fate just dropped you right in his hands. Another perfect victim."

Now she jumped to her feet and their bodies brushed. "I'm not anyone's victim." The hell she was.

"Ivy," he sighed out her name. "I've been doing research on you, too."

Only fair. She'd dug into his past and —

"Why do you like danger so much?"

She flinched at that question. "It's not the danger. Maybe I just want to help someone else." And that was exactly what she was doing — trying to help. Trying to save someone else's life.

Her grandfather had trained her well, and she'd loved working at his PI business. And it wasn't just about the rush that came from the job. It was about the difference that she could make. The difference her grandfather had made.

Her father had tried to crash and burn that legacy, but she'd been determined to build it back up. Ivy heaved out a hard breath. "Money and power can do a lot of things in this world. They can sure hide plenty of sins."

"Like your father's?"

"I know you hated him." There was no use pretending for either of them. "He blackmailed his way to power. He covered his past, made sure that the skeletons in his closet would stay dead, but *I* am not him."

"I never said you were."

"No, you just look at me sometimes, judging me, thinking I'm cut from the same cloth." Why had she thought anything would change regarding that? "Screw that, Bennett. Screw *you*." She shoved by him and marched for the door.

She'd taken only a few steps when he caught her. He grabbed her wrist and swung her back around to face him. The office was small and with their bodies intimately close — it sure felt one hell of a lot smaller.

"He got away with murder," Bennett whispered.

Yes, he had. But only for a time.

"He was drinking that night, Ivy," Bennett continued gruffly. "He *killed* her. And the cops and the media just let him walk."

She thought of that fiery crash. Of the way the flames had shot in the sky. She'd gotten there right after the accident. She and Bennett had arrived together. She'd seen the aftermath.

And had borne the brunt of Bennett's pain, even back then.

His aunt had been in that car. His aunt...she'd been the one that Senator DuLane hit with his BMW late one night after he'd had too many drinks at his bay house. His car had slammed right into hers, and Bennett's aunt...she'd never been able to escape the flames.

But the cops and the press, they'd told a different story. Slick roads. Too much rain. A tragic accident.

Not manslaughter.

No matter what Bennett and his mother had said, no one had believed them. Hell, there hadn't even been a blood alcohol test taken from the senator that night, or…if there *had* been, it had vanished later.

Money and power.

That night had torn her and Bennett apart. He'd become so angry. So full of rage. And so determined to get justice.

He'd left town. Joined the FBI.

And she'd…

Stayed. I tried to make things better. I tried to atone. It just didn't always work for me.

"I couldn't stay here," Bennett said. "Not after that. Not with the world treating him like he was some damn victim."

No.

"He tried to buy us off," Bennett admitted.

She knew this, and it broke her heart all the more.

A muscle flexed in his jaw. "My mother took that money. She took his fifty thousand, and she didn't look back."

Bennett's mother had cleared out of town and never come back. Bennett's father had died when he was a child, just as Ivy's mom had, and Bennett—

"Why did you come back?" Ivy asked. She truly hadn't thought there was anything left for him in this town.

"Don't you know?" His eyes glittered at her as his head began to lower.

Her heart beat faster. She wanted to think that he'd come back for her. That after all that time had passed, he'd still cared. He'd needed her.

But she wasn't given to delusions. Not usually, anyway.

"Why?" Ivy asked again, her voice soft.

He kissed her. Not a hard, desperate kiss. Not an I'm-Starving-And-Must-Have-You kiss. But deep. Slow. Sensual.

Her eyes closed as she leaned in to him. Ivy's mouth moved slowly against his. Her lips touched his, and her tongue slid to tease his. She'd always loved his kiss. He'd savored her in the past—and he was savoring her now.

He hadn't been the first boy she'd ever kissed, but he had been the first to teach her about passion and need.

And the first to break her heart.

I begged him to stay, for me.

Her hands rose and pressed to his chest. She pushed against him and Bennett's head slowly lifted. His eyes were heavy-lidded, that green of his gaze so very deep.

"You know I want you," Bennett said.

Wanting wasn't enough but...

Maybe it can do, for now.

"You've been in my dreams," Bennett told her, his voice gruff. "Too many nights. A man should never think about one woman the way I think about you."

"How do you think about me, exactly?" Because that would be good to know. Her own voice had come out husky.

"Every damn way I can. I think about the things I want to do with you. To you." His voice deepened even more as he confessed, "The way I feel about you...it isn't safe, Ivy. It isn't good. You should be telling me to get my hands off you."

"But I want your hands on me." All over her. "I'm not the one who ran away."

"Ivy..."

She rose onto her toes. She'd pushed him away a moment before but now she was the one locking her arms around his neck and pulling him back down to her. She'd stopped him because the kiss, while certainly good, had been wrong.

Too slow. Too careful. Too controlled.

When they touched, they were supposed to ignite. The passion was supposed to take over. It wasn't supposed to be lukewarm. *Good.*

That's the way it was with others.

With Bennett, it was supposed to be insane.

"Let go," she whispered against his mouth, and then she kissed him again—with every bit of need and desire that she had bottled up inside of her.

She let go.

And...so did he.

This kiss was different. This kiss was hot. It was wild. It made lust burn through every cell of her body. His hands were on her hips now, and he jerked her up against him. That wasn't enough. That wasn't close enough—he must have felt the same way because Bennett lifted her up. He pinned her against the nearest wall and he crushed her there, caging Ivy with his body.

His mouth didn't let hers go. His tongue, his lips—they were whipping up the frenzy of her need. Her nipples were tight and aching and she couldn't get enough of him.

Her nails sank into his shoulders. Her legs wrapped around his hips. The guy was sexy strong—he held her easily right there and—

Something was ringing.

It was her.

Bennett's head lifted. He blinked and frowned down at her.

"M-my phone," Ivy whispered. Someone had the worst timing in the entire world. Her legs slipped off his hips and her feet hit the floor, and it was a good thing he still had a grip on her waist because her knees felt a little jiggly. She fumbled and yanked her phone out of her back pocket. *Unknown caller.* She glanced at Bennett, but then put the phone to her ear. "Hello?" It was far too late for some telemarketer, and the kick in her gut warned her this wasn't going to be good.

"Why are you with him?" The voice was low, rasping. Was it the same voice that she'd heard the night before, in that dark corridor? She couldn't tell for certain. *Maybe.*

Her gaze was on Bennett. "Who is this?"

"I'm the man in the mask…the only man you should see…"

Her hand shook just a little as she held that phone. She pulled the phone from her ear and swiped her fingers over the screen, activing the speaker option so that Bennett could hear the call. She mouthed *"It's him"* to Bennett.

Ivy cleared her throat. "The man in the mask? I don't—"

"You saw me. Did you enjoy it? Knowing that she was dying, right then. With the crowd all around, but they were oblivious, so oblivious…*we* knew. You and I. Just us."

Oh, jeez, he was making it sound as if they'd been involved in the killing together. "I tried to stop you!"

He laughed. That laughter chilled her.

"Why did you kill the councilman?" Ivy asked. She wanted him to keep talking and to confess anything—everything—he could while Bennett was listening. Then, going by instinct, she said, "He wasn't a pretty young brunette, not your type at all."

"No," the caller agreed. "You're my type."

Her chill got worse.

"He was in the way. He saw me. Shined his damn light right on me. What was I supposed to do? Let him just walk away?"

"He didn't know you were a killer," Ivy argued. "You were two men in the dark."

"I had my knife out. He saw it. He knew me."

Bennett mouthed, *"Keep him talking."*

"The cops found out about your other victims. The ones here and in New Orleans. They're going to find you."

Silence.

So much for getting the guy to keep talking.

"Hello?" Ivy pushed. "Are you—"

"You're letting him hear the call, aren't you, Ivy?" He sighed, sounding disappointed. "You aren't going to trap me. That isn't the way this works." Voices rose in the background. She could hear laughter. Music? "But I *will* be trapping you. We'll be meeting again. Very, very soon."

He hung up.

"A party," Ivy muttered. "Another ball?"

Bennett didn't answer, he just spun and rushed for the door. "We're going to try and trace that call."

Could he do that? She hoped so but the knot in her stomach told her things weren't going to be so easy. This guy—if he'd been killing for years, he wasn't going to just go down with a slip-up like a traceable call. He'd probably used a burner phone or he'd stolen someone else's phone or — hell, he could have done just about anything.

No, it wasn't going to be that easy.

The guy was playing a game. He'd called so she'd know. So she'd be afraid.

I will be trapping you.

And, dammit, she was scared.

***

He slipped the phone into his pocket and smiled. Another night, another ball. And there were so many beautiful brunettes at that ball. Their dresses were lovely, glinting in the light. Whispering against their legs as the women walked.

High heels. Sexy scents.

Such tempting prey.

Not as tempting as she is.

He smiled and then pushed back through the crowd. This ball wasn't held at the convention center. No, tonight he'd chosen to attend the ball held in one of the historic mansions in downtown Mobile. A mansion with a spiral staircase and too many glittering chandeliers.

He saw the dark-haired man to his right. He bumped into the guy, mumbling his apologies even as he slipped the phone *back* into the guy's pocket. It had certainly been easy enough to take that phone minutes before.

In a crush like this, pockets were meant to be picked.

"Sorry, there, buddy," he muttered as he straightened up. "I think I've had a few too many drinks tonight."

The man smiled at him, flashing a dimple in his left cheek. "That's okay. Just be careful." His smile dimmed. "You don't want to go driving home that way."

Gravely, he shook his head. "A taxi is in my future."

The guy's dark brown eyes warmed. "Good man." He clapped a hand on his shoulder. "I'm Hugh. Hugh DuLane."

Tell me something I don't already know...

"Hell of a party, isn't it?" Hugh asked.

Yes, it was.

***

"My brother?" Ivy's lips had parted in shock. "That's not possible. That wasn't Hugh!"

The tech glanced over at Bennett, saying nothing. But then, the guy didn't need to say a word. The information on the computer screen was pretty undeniable. Thanks to the pull at the police department, they'd been able to get the phone company to hook them right up with the information they'd needed.

The caller had attempted to block his number, using the old *67 trick, but they'd still been able to trace him.

The phone belonged to *Hugh DuLane.*

Hugh, who just happened to be Bennett's size. Hugh, who just happened to have dark hair. Hugh…who just happened to have a sister who looked *exactly* like the other victims.

Fucking Hugh.

"No way," Ivy said flatly. "He would never do this! And, hell, don't you think I'd recognize my own brother's voice?"

"He was at the ball last night," Bennett reminded her.

"Yes, with me!" Her cheeks flushed and she yanked the phone from his hands. He knew that she was calling her brother even before she —

Worry slid across her face. She kept the phone near her ear, but it was obvious that Hugh wasn't answering her. "Something is wrong," Ivy said. She dropped the phone. "Hugh always takes my calls."

"Where is he?"

She began to pace. "He was going to another ball tonight. His girlfriend — Shelly is in the Maidens of Folly. They were having her party at the Melton House tonight."

Then he'd be getting his ass down to the Melton House. He knew exactly where that old mansion was — the place was often rented for wedding and parties, and he had no doubt that a big crowd would be there tonight.

"He could be in danger," Ivy said. She dialed again on the phone. "Maybe I can get Shelly..." She paused a moment, then Bennett saw her face light up. "Shelly! Shelly, it's Ivy. I need to speak with Hugh, right now." She paused and Bennett could tell by her expression that the news Shelly had just given her wasn't good. "When? No, no, please try to find him. Then call me. I'm on my way there." She glanced at Bennett. "Shelly said that he disappeared about ten minutes ago. She lost him in the crush."

Hell.

"He's not doing this," Ivy said definitely. "That bastard...last night, he mentioned Hugh to me. He said it was a shame..."

A shame?

"What if he's hurting my brother, in order to get to me?"

Or what if your brother is as screwed up as your father? And we just didn't notice it before?

Because that accident that had taken Bennett's aunt...it had happened right during Mardi Gras. Right during the madness.

Coincidence?

And, Hugh...he'd been in the back seat of his father's car. He'd seen that nightmare go down, and he'd watched his father get away with murder.

"Let's go," Bennett said.

But Ivy was ahead of him. She was already running for the door. He knew how things worked with Ivy and Hugh. No one ever came between them. He'd tried. And he'd gotten shut down real fast. Ivy would do anything for her brother.

But could she see the darkness inside of him?

CHAPTER SEVEN

"Stop sir," a big, burly bouncer ordered as he stepped into Bennett's path. His bald head gleamed under the light and a diamond winked from his right ear lobe. "Tails are required for this event." He glanced toward Ivy and shook his head. "And ma'am, you *know* those jeans won't get you inside."

Bennett lifted his badge. "How about this? Will this get us inside?"

The bouncer stepped back and smiled. "You should've mentioned you had the VIP pass," he murmured.

Bennett just nodded as he took Ivy's hand and hurried past the security check-in. Music drifted in the air, spilling out from the open doors and windows at Melton House. The mansion was on a secluded fifteen acres, and the long wrap-around porch on the second floor was filled with men and women. Some wearing masks. Some without.

He was really getting sick of the masks.

"Bennett..." Ivy stopped.

He looked back at her, only Ivy was staring up at the balcony. He followed her gaze and saw the man in the white mask and black tux. A man who seemed to be staring straight down at her.

"The men don't wear masks at this event," she said quickly. "It's a party for the women's Mardi Gras organization. They're the ones in masks, and Shelly's group picked out green masks, I saw them at her place last week."

Sonofabitch.

The man up there—he *bowed* to Ivy.

"That's him," she whispered. "Oh, my God—"

"Stop!" Bennett bellowed.

The man didn't stop. He turned on his heel and started pushing through the crowd on the balcony. "Dammit!" Bennett kept his hold on Ivy and started running toward the entrance to Melton House. That jerk had been waiting out there. He'd *wanted* Ivy to see him.

He lured her here. He lured us both here. Bennett tightened his hold on Ivy. He wasn't going to let her out of his sight.

When they burst inside the house, Bennett's gaze swept the packed scene. Ivy had been right—none of the men in the lower area of the house were wearing masks.

What is his plan? Bennett wondered as he looked around. *What does he want?* He looked up, and then Bennett raced toward the spiral staircase.

"Ivy!"

Hugh stood in the middle of that staircase. He had on a black tux, with tails, and his dark hair was pushed away from his face. He smiled at Ivy. "What are you doing here?" Hugh asked her. "You—"

Bennett's left hand slammed into the guy and he shoved Hugh against the railing.

"Bennett, no!" Ivy ordered as she tore free from him. "Stop it! My brother isn't the one you're after!"

She seemed so very certain, but then, Ivy didn't trust anyone else the way she trusted Hugh. She'd do anything for Hugh. Lie. Fight.

Leave me. Yes, he'd known that, even years ago.

"What's your problem, Detective?" Hugh demanded.

It had gotten very, very quiet on that staircase. Bennett glanced around and saw that they had nearly everyone's attention in the immediate area.

"Where is your phone?" Each word was a growl from Bennett.

Hugh just blinked. "Uh, in my pocket?"

Bennett let him go. "Give it to me. *Now.*"

Hugh pulled out his phone. "You're a crazy SOB, you know that?"

"You had this phone all night? You never let it out of your sight?"

Hugh looked around. His cheeks reddened. "You interrogating me, *now*?"

Ivy pushed against Bennett. "The man we're after is getting away!"

Was he? Bennett wasn't so sure...

***

"Hugh?" Shelly Estes rubbed her arms as she walked across the balcony on the west side of Melton House. It was dark back there, with only a few couples hiding in the shadows. Kissing. Sharing their secrets in the night.

The balcony on the east side had been a totally different story — the crush out there had been unbelievable. Probably because the band was playing closer to that balcony. It had been the place to see and be seen.

Maybe Hugh doesn't want to be seen, though. Maybe he is out here.

She put her hands on her hips. When she found Hugh, the jerk was going to get it. He didn't get to cut out in the middle of the ball, not when it was her night. Sure, she understood that he was worried about his sister, but that didn't mean the guy got to pull a vanishing act on her and —

"You're looking for Hugh DuLane?" A dark, deep voice queried from her right.

Shelly spun around. A tall, handsome man stood just a few feet away. He smiled at her, showing off perfectly straight, white teeth. "Or is there..." he murmured. "Another Hugh gone missing tonight?"

"Ah, no, I am looking for Hugh DuLane." She took a step toward him. "Have you seen him?"

"I have." His smile stretched a bit. "Want me to take you to him?"

Relief rushed through her. "Yes." Then she'd give Hugh a serious piece of her mind. *Jerk.*

He held up his hand to her. White gloves covered his fingers. She put her fingers in his. They headed back into the house.

He glanced over at her as the bright lights fell on them both and appreciation lit his gaze. *A brilliant, blue gaze.*

Shelly hesitated. "Have we met before?" Because he seemed familiar. Maybe... "Didn't I see you at the ball last night?"

His smile seemed to tighten. "Did you?"

She lifted her hand and her fingers brushed against her mask. She pulled it up so that he could see her face.

"I don't think I'd forget a lady as lovely as you."

That was nice. Hugh should say nice things like that to her.

The man's gaze seemed to linger on her hair as he said, "No, I wouldn't be able to forget a woman with hair like yours. So dark and beautiful."

She laughed at that. "Well, actually, I was a redhead last night. But I like to change things up." She'd wanted to look extra special for the ball, so a change had seemed like a good idea.

"Do you now…" He put his hand at the small of her back. Because her dress had a deep, plunging back, his gloved hand slid against her skin. A tingle of awareness pulsed through her. *This is why Hugh shouldn't abandon me at a ball. There are plenty of other handsome men who can appreciate me.*

Her smile stretched a little more. "How do you know Hugh?"

"I actually met him through his sister." He steered her toward a closed door. He opened the door, but kept his other hand on her back. "Are you well acquainted with Ivy?"

She nodded. "Why, yes, I—"

He shoved her inside and shut the door behind him.

She stumbled and nearly fell as her high heels wobbled. "Wh-what are you doing?"

He turned the lock on the door. She realized they were in some kind of storage room. And they were alone.

He reached inside of his coat and pulled out a white mask. Staring at her, he put that mask over his face.

"This isn't funny," Shelly snapped. She tried to surge around him. "I'm going back to the party."

He grabbed her, held her tight and—something sharp pressed under her chin. "You aren't going anywhere," he told her.

Her breath heaved out.

"I wasn't going to kill you…you weren't my plan." The tip of a knife slid up her chin and began to trail over her lips. "But then you said you saw me last night. I had my mask on, love. You weren't supposed to remember me."

She…she… "Your eyes," she whispered. "I remembered them." Because she'd been at the whiskey bar with Hugh and Cameron. Cameron had been talking with that man. He'd looked over at them, and she'd been caught by his eyes. Such bright, blue eyes.

Unforgettable eyes.

Eyes that she suddenly wished she'd never seen.

Shelly wanted to scream, but that blade was right at her lips. She had a horrible flash of him cutting her mouth. Of him using that knife on her…

She stopped moving.

"Are you going to be good to me, Shelly?" he asked her.

She managed a nod.

"Good. Then don't make a sound…" He moved the knife away from her lips. Her breath heaved out. Her heartbeat was drumming in her ears. Maybe if she didn't fight him, he'd just let her go. Maybe…maybe he was just going to scare her.

"I won't tell anyone," Shelly whispered as tears stung her eyes. "I promise."

He smiled at her. "I know you won't."

She tried to smile back at him.

He drove the knife into her chest. "Because the dead can't talk."

She stared up at his mask. Up at his unforgettable eyes. His eyes were the last thing she saw.

***

"This is bullshit!" Hugh snarled. "Get out of my face, *Detective* Morgan!"

Bennett just leaned closer. "You told me you had this phone with you all night. Then explain to me," he ordered, "about the phone call that Ivy got less than thirty minutes ago. A call from the killer…from the guy I heard confess to stabbing the councilman."

Hugh's face went slack with shock. "Wait…*what?*"

"If you had the phone, then *you* made the call."

"No, I didn't!" Hugh denied. His gaze swung to Ivy. "Hell, I swear it! You know I'd never do anything to hurt you!"

No, just the rest of the world.

"It wasn't Hugh." And Ivy shoved around them both as she hurried up the stairs. "And you two are wasting time. He's up there!"

Bennett glared at Hugh even as he carefully put that phone in his coat pocket. He'd run the phone for prints and see what they turned up, and in the meantime, he'd keep Hugh in sight.

Hugh tried to push past him, hurrying after Ivy.

Bennett grabbed him and barked, "You do anything to hurt Ivy, and you are a dead man." Ivy might trust her brother, but Bennett recognized the guy for exactly what he was.

Trouble.

He locked his hand in Hugh's collar and pushed the guy up ahead of him. Ivy was at the top of the stairs now, and she glanced back, glaring at them both.

She didn't see her brother for what he was — she had her blinders on with him. Always had. But Bennett wasn't blind.

"I-I need to find Shelly," Hugh mumbled. "I was going upstairs to get some air when I saw you come in."

Bennett's eyes narrowed at those words. So Hugh wanted him to believe that he hadn't been on the balcony.

"Shelly was upstairs when I saw her last," Hugh said, hurrying his steps as they neared the landing. "When we find her, she can clear everything up for me."

Bennett wasn't seeing Shelly, though. He also wasn't seeing anyone else that could have been the killer. *Just Hugh.* The other men they passed didn't match the guy's description. A few moments later, Bennett followed Ivy out onto the balcony. There were only couples out there. One man with red hair was embracing a blonde. A balding guy was slow dancing with his partner. A fellow in Navy dress blues held hands with his date.

Where is the bastard in the mask?

"He's not here," Ivy said. She hurried past him and ran back into the hallway. "We should look—"

Hugh reached out and grabbed her arm. "If the killer is here, then I want to find Shelly, now." A new urgency had entered his tone.

Ivy searched his gaze, then she nodded. She pulled out her phone and dialed quickly. "She answered me before. I'll get her again."

Hugh nodded, appearing relieved.

But...

"No answer," Ivy said as she began to walk. She kept the phone at her ear, no doubt listening to it ring, as she said, "there's another balcony around back, let's search it."

Bennett yanked Hugh after her. Bennett assessed every man they passed. He paused at the top of the stairs, his gaze trekking down below, looking for that taunting bastard. The men at this party weren't wearing masks, though. The bastard had probably just taken it off once he'd left the balcony, and then he'd blended right in with the crowd.

The thick crowd truly did make for a perfect hunting ground.

He turned away from the stairs, ready to check that other balcony. Hugh was at his side, Bennett made sure of that with his grip on the guy. They took a few quick steps forward—

Hugh froze. "That's her tone."

Ivy kept walking. She still had the phone at her ear.

"That's Shelly's ring tone!" Hugh yelled.

Ivy whirled back around.

Hugh jerked free of Bennett's hold. He put his head next to the door on the right. "I can hear it." He glanced back at Ivy. "You know she loves Katie Perry." He grabbed for the door knob and twisted, but the door didn't open. "Shelly!" Hugh called. He knocked his fist on the door. "Shelly, open up! I need you to talk with the jerk Morgan! Tell him that I've been with you."

Ivy put her phone down. Her worried gaze met Bennett's.

"Shelly?" Hugh knocked on the door again. "Come on, baby. Open the door. This isn't funny." He laughed, the sound rough and awkward. "I'm sorry that I didn't come back upstairs right away. It's just...I needed a break. The crowd was pressing in on me. I felt like everyone was staring. Watching. You know the way gossip follows my family."

There was no response from within that room. Bennett put his hand on Hugh's shoulder and pushed him back. Bennett tried the knob — definitely locked.

"Maybe it's not her," Ivy said as she approached them. The phone on the other side of that door had stopped ringing. "I'm sure Katie Perry songs are real popular ring tones."

Bennett glanced down at the phone cradled in Ivy's hands. "Call her again."

She swallowed and her fingers slid across the screen. He saw the screen note of *Dialing Shelly*...and Shelly's smiling face appeared on Ivy's screen.

Then the call connected.

And Katie Perry began to sing from behind the door.

"She could have dropped her phone," Hugh said quickly as he gave a hard nod. "I bet that's what happened. She dropped her phone in there. She's probably somewhere else, hell, maybe she's even looking for her phone..."

Bennett wasn't so sure of that, and, judging by the worry on Ivy's face, she wasn't, either. They both knew the killer was there — and he could already have a new victim.

"Get back," Bennett ordered.

"Why?" Hugh blustered. "What are you —"

Growling, Bennett pushed the guy back once more. Then he kicked in that door. If he was wrong, he'd pay for a new door. If he was right—

He saw the blood.

Shit, but he hadn't wanted to be right.

Shelly was on the floor, blood covering her gown, and a green mask was just inches from her fingers. Her mask?

Her lashes were closed, her body so still. He hurried to her, and Bennett put his fingers on her throat.

No pulse, but she was still warm. *So warm because...he just killed her.* "We need to lock this place down. No one else leaves." He surged to his feet.

"Shelly!" Hugh tried to rush past Bennett.

Bennett grabbed the guy. "No, dammit! This is a crime scene, stay back!"

But Hugh fought his hold. Twisting, and punching and when Hugh's fist slammed into his jaw, Bennett swore, but didn't let the other guy go. "You can't help her now. She's gone man, I'm sorry."

"No." Hugh's denial was sharp. "No, she's not!" He kept fighting, but Bennett pulled Hugh out of the room. "Shelly! *Shelly, baby—no!*" Pain and fear laced his voice. "Please, no," he whispered.

Bennett glanced at Ivy. Her hand was over her mouth and tears trekked down her cheeks.

"We have to get security to close this scene," Bennett said softly. "No one can leave, not until my men talk to everyone here." Because the killer was there — if the bastard hadn't already slipped away. "We close this place down, *now*."

Ivy nodded.

"Shelly?" Hugh's voice was lost. "Why...*Shelly?*"

***

"Have a good night, gentlemen," he murmured as he cleared the security gate. He gave the security staff a friendly wave as he waited for the valet to bring his car around. He didn't want to appear nervous, after all. Why would he want to do that?

He smiled at them. "Sure were some pretty women here tonight."

Shelly had been a pleasant surprise. Would they find her soon? He certainly hoped so. What fun that discovery would be.

The man to his right — a big, balding fellow who was built rather like a tank — gave him a broad smile. "Plenty of pretty women," the guy agreed. A diamond winked from his ear lobe.

And, because it tempted him so much, he just had to tell the man, "There was one brunette there..." He whistled. "She was to die for."

The valet appeared, driving up in the Porsche.

Such a beautiful ride. One that commanded attention. Just like he commanded attention.

The smile was still on his lips as he climbed into the driver's seat. He handed off his tip to the valet.

And he heard the crackle of a radio to the right. He glanced over, idly curious. The bald guard with the earring pulled the radio away from the clip on his hip.

"This is Morris," he said.

"We're under lockdown…a detective is saying that no one should – "

Ah, that would be his cue to leave. "Have a good night." He closed his door, pushed his foot down on the gas pedal and got the hell out of there before Morris's boss could finish giving him instructions. Instructions that he was sure originated from Detective Bennett Morgan.

You found her.

Much faster than he'd thought. Yes, it was definitely time to leave this particular party. And he was getting away clean. The way he always did.

CHAPTER EIGHT

Ivy hunched her shoulders when the body was brought out of Melton House. She was getting really tired of seeing dead bodies.

Only that wasn't just any dead body...

I've known Shelly for years. They'd shared secrets. Laughter. Tears. Shelly had always been trailing after Hugh, and her brother had finally gotten his shit together and seen the beautiful woman who wanted him.

Now she was gone.

Ivy shivered in the night air.

Dozens of cops were at the scene. Police tape blocked the driveway—so did armed guards. No one was getting out of that ball without talking to the cops. They were getting names and addresses. They were questioning everyone for details about that night.

And her brother...he was one of the ones being grilled the most.

Hugh was currently in the back of a patrol car. The door was open, and another detective—Drew Trout—was leaning in close, talking to him. Grilling him.

It's not Hugh.

Bennett should understand that. He needed to get his colleague to understand that the killer had tried to set up Hugh. That he'd used Hugh's phone.

That he'd killed Hugh's lover.

Her gaze slid back to the body bag.

I'm so sorry, Shelly.

"No, no, I'm telling you…" A man's voice rose, drawing her attention to the left. "I shut the place down as soon as I got the radio message from my boss."

Her body turned toward that voice. She saw Bennett with his arms crossed, sizing up one of the security guards at the event — the guy they'd passed when they'd first arrived. Big, tough, with a gleaming bald head and good taste in diamonds.

"No one got out of here after I got that message," the guy said flatly. "My boys and I secured the scene. No one got past us then."

She inched closer to them.

"Did anyone leave right before that?" Bennett asked.

The fellow sputtered and said, "Yeah, folks been coming and going all night. I didn't know to stop them!"

Bennett's hands fell to his side. "Morris, I need to know if a man left. A man about my size with dark hair. I think he would have been traveling alone."

Morris's gaze slid away from his. The guy seemed to be staring over near the valet line. A line that wasn't moving very much at all.

"He said," Morris licked his lips, "he said the brunette...that she was 'to die for'..."

Ivy swallowed as nausea rose within her.

"Who said that?" Bennett asked immediately.

"The guy — the guy who drove off in the Porsche. Real sweet ride." Morris ran a hand over the top of his head. "He was your height. Had his tux coat tucked under his arm."

Because he was hiding some blood that might have gotten on it?

"I need a full description of him." Bennett's voice was grim.

"I-I didn't know to stop him. Not then. He was friendly. Not in any kind of rush. I mean, if he'd just killed that lady..." Now the bouncer's gaze slid toward the ME's van. His jaw locked. "Shouldn't he have been running?"

Not him. He's too cool. Too controlled.

"Describe him," Bennett said.

"White guy, dark hair, blue eyes. Shit — I don't know. His hair was pushed back. I just — I really noticed the car, okay? It was a sweet ride. Damn fine. I was looking more at it than I was at him."

Bennett motioned to a nearby officer who hurried over. Then Bennett focused on the witness again. "Did you get the tag number?"

"Uh…"

No, he hadn't. Ivy could already tell that from the man's tone of voice.

Bennett turned to the uniform. "There's a traffic camera at the light two blocks away. Get access to that camera, *now*. If the Porsche is on there, we can get the license plate." He pointed at Morris. "And you're going to describe the vehicle to us. Every detail. We'll get an APB out on the car. I want every Porsche fitting that description pulled over right the fuck now. The guy wants to drive a fancy ride? His mistake. It will just make tracking him easier."

Maybe…Ivy shifted a bit nervously from foot to foot as she considered the matter.

But the killer had stolen Hugh's phone to call her.

So maybe he'd just stolen that car from someone, too. Just in case…in case a situation like this occurred. If his car was spotted, he wouldn't want it to be traced back to him.

"It was dark blue," Morris said quickly. "A new car, one of those fancy 911 models."

Oh, hell. Ivy cleared her throat. She had to speak up now. "I know someone with a car like that."

Bennett's gaze was immediately on her.

"Cameron Wilde," she said softly. "He got that 911 just a few months ago." He'd been so proud of that car, driving it everywhere. Then he'd gotten a scratch on it when the car had been parked at a wine bar. After that, he'd started keeping his ride locked up in his garage, and taking his "baby" out only for special occasions.

"Was Cameron attending the party tonight?" Bennett asked her.

"I don't think so. When I talked to him last…" A talk that hadn't gone so well. "He said he was heading over to his beach house. He has a place in Fort Morgan." That would be about an hour drive away. "If his plans changed, he didn't tell me." *And he wouldn't.* Because he'd been pissed when he left her.

"I'm putting out an APB for that car," Bennett said, his voice hard. "And I want you…" His gaze cut back to Morris once more. "I want you going downtown."

Morris lifted his hands. "Aw, man, no, I—"

"You're working with a sketch artist. You saw the guy. You—and any of your men who were close by. I want every single detail that you can give me. This man has killed three people in the last two days. He's not getting away with his crimes."

Because if they didn't catch him, Ivy knew he'd just be killing someone else again soon.

"And I want a patrol car sent to Cameron Wilde's house, right now," Bennett gritted out as the officer near him nodded briskly. "Bring him in to the station. I'll be having a nice chat with him, too."

"Bennett—" Ivy began.

He whirled toward her. He took two steps and his hands caught her shoulders. "It could have been you in that body bag."

She shook her head.

"He called *you*. He lured *you* here. He's baiting us. Playing a game that I won't let him win." His breath sawed out as his eyes glittered down at her. "I won't let you be his victim. I can't." His hold tightened on her. "I need you too much."

That was good, right? He needed her. He—

"So I'm sorry, Ivy, but this has to be done. You matter too much. I can't risk you." He dropped his hands and stepped back.

Oh, no. She got a very bad feeling in the pit of her stomach. "Bennett?" Just what was he doing?

Bennett sighed. "Officer Jansen, please place Ivy DuLane in protective custody."

"What?" Had she just misheard? Because she was already freaking out over Shelly, so maybe—

"You're going to have a guard, twenty-four seven, until this bastard is caught." Bennett's hands clenched at his sides. "You're not going in a body bag, understand? I won't let that happen. I've seen first-hand what sick freaks like him do to their prey. How they get off on the pain. That's not happening to you. It can't." His voice sounded ragged as he whirled away from her.

Seriously—that was it? "Bennett?" Chill bumps rose on her arms.

"Um, Ms. DuLane?" A female officer was at her side. Must be Officer Jansen. She hadn't even realized the woman was there until Bennett had said the lady's name. "You'll need to come with me now."

Bennett had already paced several feet away. He was on his phone, barking orders. Probably demanding that APB and putting out a search for Cameron.

"Can he do that?" Ivy asked. "Can he just put me in protective custody?"

"Uh, ma'am, it's for your safety."

The ME's van was pulling away. *Shelly didn't have any chance of safety.* She shouldn't have died. If the killer was truly playing a game…*then why won't he just come after me?* Why was he bringing her friends and her brother into this nightmare?

"Life can change so fast," Ivy murmured. "Two days ago, my biggest worry was whether or not I'd get enough new clients this year for my business."

Now…

Now she had to worry about staying alive. Worry about protecting those close to her.

If he wants me, then he needs to focus on me. And leave them the hell alone.

"Ma'am," Officer Jansen's voice hardened. "You need to come with me now."

Ivy nodded. Yes, she did. And she also needed to figure out what the hell she could do next.

***

Police Chief Berney Quarrel stalked into Bennett's office and shut the door behind him with a soft click. "Tell me...*please* tell me that I didn't see Senator DuLane's son in my interrogation room."

Bennett put down his phone. "You saw him."

The chief winced. "You really thinking that man is our killer? That he brutally stabbed his own girlfriend and then just hung around at that party, waiting for her body to be found?"

I think Hugh DuLane has plenty of secrets.

"You think that man is harassing his own sister? Trying to kill *her?*"

"No, shit, I don't." Because Bennett thought the man they were after had driven away in a Porsche. "I saw Hugh when he realized Shelly Estes was dead." The guy had been destroyed. And Bennett didn't think that reaction had been faked. "He's just one of the killer's pawns. Hell, the guy is *in* interrogation because I think *he* saw the bastard. I think the guy walked right up to Hugh and took his phone, and DuLane didn't even realize what was happening."

The chief grunted. "Well, that makes things easier. At least I won't have to deal with the nightmare of arresting a *DuLane*."

Even with the scandals that had been attached to their family, Bennett knew the name still carried power. Power and too much wealth.

"Would it matter?" Bennett asked him grimly. "Say Hugh was our killer. Would his last name stop you from arresting the guy?" Because the senator hadn't been arrested when he'd committed murder. Back then, the cops had just let him walk.

The chief's face hardened. "You must not know me well, son. Because you shouldn't have to ask that question." His coal black eyes narrowed. "Money and power don't mean shit to me if you're guilty."

Good. Bennett nodded. "My apologies, sir."

The chief grunted. "You think I don't know about what went down here before? I heard all about your aunt."

That wasn't what Bennett had expected to hear right then.

"That shit won't go down under my command. Count on it."

Bennett's respect for the man notched up even more.

"Now tell me about Cameron Wilde," the chief said gruffly.

He wished that he had more to say. "You know Cameron Wilde is missing."

The chief lowered into Bennett's desk chair.

"Wilde *and* the Porsche." The traffic camera had caught that vehicle fleeing, and they'd gotten the tag number, a tag number that showed the owner of the vehicle was one Cameron Wilde.

His hair isn't dark. It's blond. But, otherwise... "There weren't any signs of foul play at his house in Mobile. Ivy told me the guy had a second home over at the Fort Morgan beach area. I had officers from the Fort Morgan police department check the place out, but they said it looked deserted." Not a good sign. "They're going to head back at first light and check again." Though they sure hadn't sounded very hopeful when they'd talked to him.

"How are those sketches going?" Chief Quarrel asked him.

"Fucking worthless." He shook his head. "We had three witnesses who saw the guy — Morris Hatch, the head of the security at the gate, a guy named Todd Wiles, and Peter Blask, the valet. All three men saw the driver of that Porsche. And when they were paired up with sketch artists, all damn three of them described a different man. The pictures are useless to me."

The chief sighed. "You know how faulty eye witness descriptions can be — especially in situations like this one."

Yeah, he damn well knew how unreliable such testimony could be. He'd had his share of issues with misleading descriptions during his time with the FBI. But he'd hoped they'd gotten lucky. He'd *needed* to see who he was hunting.

"I've got the APB out for Wilde," Bennett said. "Uniforms are searching his property and his business. We should be able to find him."

The chief just looked back at him.

And Bennett knew the chief was thinking the same thing he was. *We should be able to find him...provided that Cameron Wilde was still alive.*

He wasn't so sure about that. Maybe the killer had stabbed Cameron and dumped his body, *then* taken his ride.

"You're the hotshot from the FBI," the chief groused. "I know you worked with serials. Is that what we've got here? A serial?"

Bennett's hand rose and pressed to his side. Beneath his shirt, he could just feel the ridge of his scar. So many scars marked him. "Usually, serials have certain victim types that they enjoy."

"Like pretty young brunettes..."

"Just like that."

The chief's fingers tapped on Bennett's desk. "Give me a profile."

Bennett's brows rose. "I'm not a profiler, not some psychiatrist—"

"Aw, cut the bullshit. You were Violent Crimes. I know you're the one who tracked down the Greenville Trapper."

Bennett didn't let his expression alter. *Greenville Trapper.* That was the name the media had come up with for the killer who had terrorized the Greenville, South Carolina area. A man who'd hunted his prey—and had trapped that prey. The Trapper had seen himself as some sort of big gamesman, and he'd only gone after big prey. Men in their prime. Men who were physically fit. Men who could survive his game for longer periods of time.

Because after he'd trapped his prey, the sick freak had enjoyed torturing them…for weeks.

"I tracked him," Bennett said grimly. The marks beneath his clothes—the scars he would always carry—seemed to burn.

"So I think you know a pretty good bit about profiling killers." The chief motioned to him. "Profile this one. Go—"

Bennett's door flew open. Ivy stood there, chest heaving, her dark eyes blazing at him. "Three hours," she snapped.

What was she doing there? She was—

"I've been back in holding for three hours." She stalked toward him and jabbed her finger into his chest. "Like a common criminal! I'm all for protective custody. I mean, hell, do what you need to do, but you can't just lock me up and forget about me!"

As if he could forget about her.

"You need to use me," Ivy said flatly. "The killer is calling me. He's hurting my friends—*use me*."

The fuck he would.

"Ah, Ms. DuLane," the chief murmured as he rose. "I was wondering when you'd be making an appearance."

Ivy glanced over at him. "As exciting as I find your jail, Chief. I think my time can be better spent elsewhere."

"Actually," the chief drawled. "I think you might be here just in time. Detective Morgan was just about to tell me what sort of profile he had for the killer."

"He was?" Ivy asked quickly.

"Uh, chief, she's a civilian. She—"

"Do you have any idea how many cold cases the woman has solved in the last year?" The chief marched toward Bennett. "I tried to draft her for my force, but she likes playing it independent. Just like her grandfather."

And he suddenly wondered if—like Dr. Battiste—the chief had enjoyed fishing with Ivy's grandfather back in the day.

"He would have been proud of you," the chief murmured to Ivy.

"I don't know about that," she whispered, her voice so low that Bennett barely heard her words. But then Ivy straightened her shoulders. "Give us the profile, Bennett, and then let's see what we can do to trap him."

Trap him.

For an instant, Bennett remembered pain. Screams. Death.

"Bennett?" Ivy frowned at him. "Are you okay?"

No, he hadn't been okay in a very long time.

When he'd been far too close to death, when his partner had been dead around him, the Greenville Trapper—a guy with the non-threatening name of Paul Friend—had tried to make Bennett beg. He'd tried to break him.

Bennett had screamed with his agony, but he hadn't broken.

Because he'd been thinking…

Of her.

"He's obsessed," Bennett said flatly. "A woman…a woman he can't let go. A woman he wants to own."

Ivy stared up at him.

"Dark hair, mid-twenties…beautiful."

You won't touch her.

"He's been killing a while. So confident. The first time he killed…it was *her*." His obsession. "And he got high from the pleasure of taking her life. Of having the ultimate control. He liked that feeling. He liked having her…so he did it again and again…but he was smart. He picked two different towns. He killed when the crowds were at their full height. When the cops were so busy that they didn't notice a woman missing. He did that, not too often, maybe once a year or once every two years, controlling himself as much as possible. Choosing his victims and hunting."

Ivy licked her lower lip. "But he's had more than one victim this year."

Yes, he had. "Because something changed in his equation. *You* changed things."

"Th-that's why he called me. Why he's targeting my friends. Because I saw him kill Evette."

Yes. "Maybe he liked that you saw. Maybe it pissed him off. I don't know yet—but you were a trigger for him. You broke his control. He's acting on impulse now, with no cooling off period between his kills, and that makes him even more dangerous."

The chief rubbed his chin. "Because that means we don't know what he'll do next?"

Bennett nodded. "We need to contact the FBI. They'll send a team down here. He's been crossing state lines, killing for years. He's a serial they need to chase."

Ivy grabbed his arm. "You *were* FBI! You can catch him. Bennett, come on, we can do this."

"You're out of your league, Ivy." She didn't understand. "What will you do if he gets you alone again? If you can't get free? When he drives his knife into you...*what will you do?*"

Die.

He couldn't let that happen.

"If he's focused on me, if I set him off, then we can use that," she said desperately. "Bennett, we can—"

"He'll kill you! He'll stab you, carve you up until nothing is left!" His fury and fear erupted. "Then what the fuck am *I* supposed to do?"

She sucked in a sharp breath and pulled her hand away from him.

Silence.

"Yeah…" The chief murmured. "I'll let you two talk this out a bit more. I think I'll head in there and see what her brother has to say…"

Ivy didn't speak, not until the chief closed the door behind him.

Then…

"What the fuck," Ivy asked softly, "am *I* supposed to do if he targets someone else that I care about?"

He flexed his fingers. He wanted to touch her. Wanted to hold her tight.

"If he calls me again, if he contacts me…*we* bait the trap," Ivy said as her dark gaze held his. "Stop looking at this from a personal angle. If you didn't know me, if you'd never slept with me…wouldn't you already be using me to catch him?"

His hand lifted and slid under her chin. "I do know you. I did sleep with you." Too long ago. He needed her *now*. "And I will be lost if he hurts you."

"Bennett?" She stared at him in confusion, as if she didn't know him.

When she was the only one he'd ever let close. "How do you think I survived before?

When that freak had me chained up in that cabin? When he took his time slicing the skin from my chest even as my partner's dead body was just a few feet away?"

She backed up a step. "I didn't...I didn't know!"

She'd asked for the gritty details before. *Be careful what you wish for.* "That's what you're asking for, baby. You're asking to become a serial killer's toy. You're asking me to stand back and let that shit happen to you." He gave a grim shake of his head. "No, it won't happen. It *can't* happen."

"Bennett..."

"That's my worst fear," he rasped. "For you to be hurt like that. For you to be trapped, to need me..."

"Protective custody," she said softly. "Now I understand." She threw her arms around him.

He bent, hugging her, holding her as tightly as he could.

He thought of the way Hugh had reacted when he'd seen Shelly's body. The guy had been destroyed.

If Ivy had been on that floor...

"It can't happen," he said flatly. "It won't." Because he truly would go mad. She didn't get it—Ivy thought he'd left town and never given her another thought.

But she'd been on his mind. Every day. The one thing that had been *his*.

A knock sounded at his door. Hell, probably the chief, trying to get him moving.

He pulled away from Ivy, just a bit, and glanced at the door. Sure enough, the chief poked his head inside.

"Chief, I—" Bennett began.

"Call it a night," the chief ordered. "Go take Ms. DuLane home. You both need to catch a few hours' sleep. Then you can come back here. We'll meet at 0700."

Take her home? The hell, *no.* "But she's in custody—"

"I didn't say it had to be her home, now did I?" The chief turned away. "Priorities are important in this world, Bennett. Make sure yours are in place—and that they are the right ones."

Ivy is my priority. Priority One. Maybe it was time he proved that to her.

"Come on." He grabbed his keys and looped his fingers with hers. They hurried into the hallway and turned toward the bullpen.

But Ivy stopped and glanced back toward interrogation. "My brother?"

And then Hugh appeared. Standing in the hallway, with his shoulders hunched, her brother seemed like a completely different man to Bennett.

Ivy pulled from Bennett and hurried to Hugh's side. She wrapped her arms around him and held on tight. "I'm so sorry," Ivy said.

Hugh didn't hug her back. He stood there, stiff and seemingly lost, in her embrace.

Ivy eased back. "Hugh?"

He blinked and looked at her. Bennett didn't even know if the guy was really seeing her or not. When he'd interrogated Hugh, he'd thought the other man might be in shock. "It's my fault, isn't it?" Hugh asked.

Bennett tensed.

"Payback. Fucking karma. Because I kept my damn mouth shut before, I'm being punished now." Hugh's gaze cut to Bennett. "He was my father, man. I...he said we'd lose everything."

Bennett could barely breathe as he realized just *what* Hugh was talking about. Another time. Another murder.

"I tried to get her out of the fire."

They weren't talking about Shelly, not even close. But Shelly's death had pushed Hugh over some sort of edge.

"That's why I have the burns." Hugh looked down at his palms, and, sure enough, there were old scars there. "I tried to get to her, but she wasn't moving inside her car. He told me she was already dead."

Bennett felt his cheeks ice.

"He pulled me back. He was on his phone, calling for help. The flames were rising." Hugh closed his eyes. "Then I saw her move. Your aunt was still alive."

No, shit, no. I can't hear this now!

His aunt had been so close to him. His mother had usually been too busy with her lovers to give him much thought. But his aunt...she'd been everything.

"The car exploded before I could get back to her. I'm so sorry." Hugh raked his hands over his face. "It's payback! I let her die, and now Shelly...Shelly is gone! I didn't get to help her, either! I didn't get to do a damn thing!"

Ivy hugged him again. "Hugh, this isn't about you. It's not your fault."

He squeezed her, wrapping his arms tightly around her. "No? Then whose fault is it, Ivy? Who the hell do I blame?" Over Ivy's shoulder, Hugh met Bennett's stare.

"You blame the killer," Bennett told him. "When we catch him, when we lock that perp behind bars...*you blame him.*"

"I'm sorry," Hugh told him. "For so much...dammit, man, *I'm sorry.*"

Bennett inclined his head toward Hugh.

"Don't you wish you could change the past? Past..." Hugh's head sagged forward as he pressed closer to Ivy. "Present and future." Then he whispered something to Ivy.

Bennett didn't know what the guy had said, but Ivy jerked away from him. "No!"

Hugh smiled, a sad sight.

"No, don't ever say that! You're nothing like him! You never were!" She shook her brother, hard, and her voice rang out as she said, "You matter. You have always mattered, and I don't care what crap he told you. Our father was one grade A bastard." Then, softer, she said, "You know you matter to me."

Hugh's fingers slid under her chin. "Wait until Bennett tells you what I did. See if you still feel the same way."

All the secrets are coming out.

Hugh exhaled and focused on the uniformed cop who waited a few feet behind him. "I get my own guard, Ivy. Good deal, right? Don't worry. I'm sure he'll make certain I don't do anything too crazy." He turned and headed toward the cop.

"I'll be pissed if you do!" Ivy threatened. "I know you're hurting, Hugh, and I'm so sorry."

He glanced back at her. "I loved her, Ives."

Ives. It had been so long since Bennett had heard that nickname.

"I didn't even realize it," Hugh said as he shuffled away. "Not until I saw her on that floor."

"Hugh…" There was so much sorrow in Ivy's voice. "Please, promise me…" Her words trailed away.

But Hugh had stopped.

"Promise me you won't do anything to hurt yourself," Ivy said, "Not like…not like our father. *Promise me.*"

Bennett hurt for them both.

Hugh slowly glanced at her.

"I'll come with you," Ivy said quickly. "I'll stay with you tonight. I'll—"

"No, not tonight." Hugh's voice was firm, his eyes grief-stricken. "Tonight, I want to think of her." His jaw hardened. "And I give you my promise, Ives. I won't be like him."

Him. Their father...the all-powerful senator...a man who'd killed himself one hot southern night.

Ivy nodded. "I'll...I'll come to you tomorrow?"

Hugh nodded. Then the cop led him away.

Bennett put his hand on her shoulder.

She stiffened. "Let me guess. My brother is getting protective custody, too, right?"

"Yes."

"Good. I want him safe." She glanced back. "In case you didn't realize it, our father spent most of his time making Hugh think he was worthless." Her lips twisted. "Is it really such a surprise that when he was eighteen, Hugh caved to my dad's pressure? That he lied at the scene of that terrible accident?"

It hadn't been an accident.

The senator had truly gotten away with murder. But not forever...eventually, the guilt had set in, and then, one night, he'd put a gun in his mouth.

When Bennett had heard the news, he knew that he should have felt relief. His aunt had gotten justice. But he hadn't felt relief. He'd just felt sadness. And he'd wanted to see Ivy.

But when I got down here, she wasn't alone. She was with Cameron.

Now Cameron was missing.

***

Ivy hadn't returned home.

He sat in her bedroom, waiting. He'd been waiting for the last few hours.

But she hadn't come back home.

Her brother was a fool. The idiot had saved her security system's passcode on his phone. It had been merely a matter of a little finger swiping, and he'd had perfect access to Ivy's house.

He'd explored all the nooks and crannies.

He'd touched the silk of her underwear. He'd spread out in her bed. He'd imagined all of the wonderful things that he would do with the sensual Ivy.

Now, so much made sense to him. She'd been the piece of the puzzle that he hadn't realized was missing. A puzzle piece that had been deliberately kept from him.

She was everything now.

Every single fucking thing.

She'd be home again. Sooner or later, and when she was...

She's mine. He had so many wonderful plans for her.

CHAPTER NINE

She hadn't been to Bennett's place before. Ivy stood just inside the doorway, far too conscious of him as he closed and locked the front door. There was a quick beep as he reset the alarm.

He flipped on the lights and illumination flooded the area. Bennett's home was in the midtown area of Mobile, nestled at the end of an oak-lined street. Most of the houses in midtown were historic, and his home was no exception. The gleaming hardwood was strong and sturdy beneath her feet, and she knew the ceilings were easily thirteen feet high. The place was sparsely furnished, but the home was absolutely beautiful. Obviously, someone had spent a lot of time and dedication restoring the home.

She headed toward the fireplace. Her fingers trailed over the mantel. "Did you do the restoration yourself?"

"Yes."

Something they had in common. She'd been doing all of the painstaking work in her house, too.

"When you're not hunting criminals…" She looked back at him. "Maybe you can drop by my house and give me a hand." She thought her words might lighten the heavy tension that seemed to hang in the air between them.

But Bennett didn't smile. She didn't blame him. She didn't exactly feel like smiling either. Her eyes burned from the tears she'd already shed for Shelly.

I keep picturing her body — all of that blood. And that wasn't how she wanted to remember Shelly. She wanted to remember her friend beautiful. Happy.

"It's okay to cry," Bennett said softly.

Ivy swept the back of her hand over her cheek. "I've cried plenty. I don't want to do that anymore." Because she was afraid if she started again, the tears wouldn't stop. Grief wasn't what she wanted.

No, what she wanted, what she needed, was an escape. Something to numb the pain.

Bennett.

Her gaze met his. Held his. Could he read the need in her stare? Could he understand how much she'd changed? Everything had altered for her when she'd seen Shelly's body. Playing it safe, going slowly with him this time around — *why?* Ivy didn't know how much time they had. A killer was stalking her. She might not have tomorrow. She might have nothing but this moment.

And with the danger growing, Ivy didn't want regrets.

I want Bennett.

He seemed to understand because his green gaze darkened as he stared at her. Then, slowly, so slowly, he stalked toward her. "You have a choice to make."

Ivy waited.

"You can sleep in the guest room down the hall. You can rest and know that you're safe. Totally protected."

Her breath came a little faster. "That's option one." She nodded. "And option two?" *I don't want option one.* With option one, she'd be alone. She'd see Shelly in her mind. She'd hurt.

"Option two...you can let me have you."

Her whole body got warm.

"And you can have me." He stopped in front of her, but Bennett didn't touch her. Even though she wanted him to, so badly. "I know you said things were going too fast before, when we were at your place."

Oh, jeez...had that just been...*last night?* It had been, and, with the brutal events of the day, all of her priorities had shifted. She wanted to reach out and grab tight to her dreams. To reach for the thing she wanted most—

And I will. Why be afraid? Life was short and hard and so very unfair. People had to grab their happiness when they could, and hold on tight with both hands.

"But I don't think it's too fast," Bennett said. "I think it's just the opposite. I think things are too slow because I've wanted you back in my bed for *years* but I was too damn big of a fool to tell you."

Hope bloomed within her. Maybe it wasn't too late. Maybe—

"You need to know all of me, before you make the choice. Because there won't be any going back." Then, staring at her, he took off his coat. Tossed it aside. He still wore his gun holster, but, carefully, he removed it. Then he reached around her and put the gun on the mantel.

He still didn't touch her.

She needed his hands on her.

He exhaled slowly, then Bennett lifted up his t-shirt. He hesitated, only briefly, then tossed the shirt to the floor. "I'm not the man you knew before."

Scars sliced over his chest and stomach. So many scars. Deep, long. Twisting. All over his front torso and—

Bennett turned to show her his back.

And on his back.

Tears stung her eyes.

"The Greenville Trapper kept me for two days before I was able to kill the bastard."

She stepped toward him. His back was still to her, so he didn't see her hand trembling as she reached toward him.

"By then, he'd more than left his mark on me, physically and mentally."

Her fingers touched the deep scar on his right shoulder. It looked as if someone had just taken a knife and cut out a chunk of his skin. "Bennett..."

"I don't want your pity." His voice was sharp.

She shook her head.

"He made me into a monster, Ivy."

Her lips pressed to the scars. First one, then another. Another. "You're not a monster."

He stiffened. "I am." His voice was so stark. "And if anything happened to you, the whole world would truly see just how screwed up I am."

Tears were sliding down her cheeks. He'd endured so much. The pain—it made her sick. Made her furious. Made her want to kill.

I could have lost him. He went through this hell...and I had no idea. She pressed another kiss to his skin. His arms were clean, no scars there.

"Ivy..." He turned toward her and her gaze shot up to meet his. When he saw the tears on her cheeks, his expression hardened. "No, dammit, no, don't—"

"Shut up," she said as the tears just came harder. "You should have called me! I needed to know." She grabbed him and held tight. "I needed to know!"

Silence.

And…

"I wasn't in any shape to call anyone, baby. I was drugged up for days. More dead than alive."

He was gutting her.

"But, later, the nurses told me…I kept saying one name, again and again."

It almost hurt for her to breathe.

"Your name, Ivy. Yours. You're the thing that got me through, Ivy. The reason I survived that hell. I couldn't die because I knew I needed to come back to you."

"Bennett?"

"You're the reason I came back to Mobile. The reason I walked away from the Bureau. You were the thing that mattered to me, and I just had to figure out how the hell to get back in your life. I had to try and figure out a way to make up for the past. I was a stupid kid back then. Hurting too much. Feeling too much pain. And I pushed away the one person I should have been pulling close."

He wasn't pulling her close. He was just—

Still wiping away her tears.

"I came back because I wanted to be with you, but when I got here…I didn't know how to approach you. Didn't know what the fuck to do. I thought you were with Cameron. You two always seemed to be together—"

"Not like that." Just the one time. The mistake that still dodged her.

His chin lifted. He caught her hands and pulled them from his shoulders. Then he just—held her wrists. Between them. "I changed. I realized just how much when I got back here. Dammit, baby, I would go to your house and stand outside, watching the lights in your windows. Watching you."

He—

"That shit isn't normal. I knew then just how far I'd fallen. I wanted you too much. I needed you too much. You were my lifeline, and I was too dangerous because I couldn't stand the thought of anyone else being close to you." His jaw hardened. "When I saw you go out with Cameron, I wanted to beat the hell out of that guy. *That* isn't normal. It's not safe."

He took a step back.

She wanted to follow him. She didn't. She...

"What makes you think I'm safe?" Ivy asked. "You think you're the only one with inner demons?"

"You haven't killed a man, Ivy. I have. With my bare hands."

She flinched. "Your own life was on the line! Stop this! Stop it!" And she did follow him. Her body brushed against his. "Stop saying you're some kind of terrible person! You survived hell! Yes, you're different. How could you not be? But do you think I don't...do you honestly think I don't want you anymore?"

The answer was plain to see on his face.

"Oh, Bennett...I never stopped wanting you." *I never will.* "So tell me about that option two because that's the option I want to take."

She saw the change sweep over his face—the desperate need, the desire that wasn't checked any longer. His control shattered and he reached for her.

His hands were rough. So were hers. He kissed her with a wild, fierce lust that she craved. She couldn't get close enough to him. Her hands slid over his back, over the scars that he shouldn't have ever been forced to carry. She touched every inch of his body that she could. She needed him to understand that she still wanted him—every single bit of him.

His hands curled around her waist and he lifted her up, holding her so easily. Her legs wrapped around his hips and she felt the long, hard length of his arousal pressing against her. She arched against him, hating that her clothes were in the way. She needed them gone. Needed his jeans gone.

Flesh to flesh.

Sex to sex.

He started walking, still holding her, and a thrill shot through her. His strength had always been a turn-on for her. But then, nearly everything about him turned her on.

She began to kiss her way over his hard jaw, over the rough stubble there, then down his neck.

He growled. "Ivy…"

"Still like that, huh?" And she nipped his neck, lightly, then licked the mark. "Good to know." Her heart was drumming in her chest, her whole body going molten.

They were in his darkened bedroom now. With his elbow, he hit the light switch, flooding the room with illumination. A few more steps and he lowered her onto the bed.

She sat up quickly and, with her eyes on his, she yanked off her shirt.

She saw his green gaze darken. Ivy smiled. Then she unhooked her bra and tossed it toward him. Bennett caught her bra and fisted his fingers around it. "You are so damn perfect."

No, she wasn't. She was far, far from perfect.

She kicked away her shoes. Then Ivy lifted up her hips and pushed out of her jeans and her underwear. The last of her clothes hit the floor with a soft rustle of sound. She stretched out on the bed, completely naked and not even the slightest bit hesitant.

Not now.

Not with him.

She could feel Bennett's gaze sliding over her. Ivy swallowed, then licked her lips, wishing she could taste him. She heard the hiss of his zipper and a moment later, his jeans were the ones hitting the floor. The bed dipped beneath his weight as he closed the distance between them.

She held her breath a moment, waiting, eager, desperate to feel his touch.

But his fingers didn't trail over her skin. His thighs didn't push between hers. Instead, his mouth pressed to her shoulder. The gentlest of caresses.

"So soft," he whispered. Then he kissed her shoulder again. Her hands slid out and grabbed the covers, fisting it when she felt his lips press to her collarbone. "I fucking missed you, Ivy."

Her eyes squeezed shut. *And I missed you.*

Bennett's legs pushed between hers. She could feel the hot, hard length of his arousal against her. And his mouth—it was on her breast. His lips closed around her nipple and he sucked her in deep.

Her breath left her in a quick gasp and her hold tightened on those covers. He was licking her breast, laving her nipple with his tongue, and her hips twisted wildly against the bed as arousal flooded through her.

His hand slid down her stomach. Her eyes opened when his fingers—long, strong, slightly rough—slid between her legs.

"I want to feel you, all of you," Bennett growled.

Have at it.

He slid one finger into her. Then another. Her head tipped back as she gasped out his name. He was going so slowly. Working in and out, thrusting with his fingers even as his thumb flexed over the center of her need.

Her desire was building — strengthening with every second that passed. He was savoring her, but she wanted his wildness. She wanted *him.*

Maybe it was time to shatter his control. Maybe it was time to let their desire take over.

She let go of the covers. She grabbed him. *"Bennett."*

His head lifted. His eyes gleamed.

She pushed against his shoulders, and he rolled, lying back against the mattress. She climbed on top of him, straddling his hips. "It's been too long."

"Yes…"

She pushed her sex over him. She was wet and ready and she wanted him inside.

She bent her head and licked his nipple. Bennett hissed out a breath. Good, so good…

But they could do better. His hands reached for her, but she grabbed them and pushed them back against the bed. "No, I get to touch now."

And she was touching all of him. Licking his flat nipples. Kissing the scars that sliced down his stomach. Moving on down, down to the heavy length of his arousal. Her fingers curled over him. Her mouth pressed to him —

"Ivy." It was a guttural demand.

She ignored it. She savored. She took. She — Was on her back. He was over her.

"Don't. Move." Such a fierce, hot demand.

One she ignored. Because when he leaned to the side, reaching for the nightstand drawer, she ran her hands over his chest and she felt the quick, hard flex of his muscles.

"Ivy." A warning edge entered his voice.

She ignored the warning and pressed a kiss to his skin.

He pulled away from her.

"No!" Ivy cried. He'd better not be stopping.

But then she saw that he was just ripping open the foil packet he'd grabbed, and when he had the protection in place, he reached for her again. He caught her hands and pinned them above her head. "You have trouble following orders," Bennett said, his voice a sensual rasp.

Guilty.

"Let's see if you can follow this order." He kept her wrists imprisoned with one hand while his other moved down her body. Stroked her sex. Then Bennett positioned his cock at the entrance of her body. "I want you to come for me, Ivy."

She planned to ignite for the guy. She planned—

He thrust into her. Deep and hard and he stretched every inch of her sex. Her breath left her in a quick rush as her whole body stiffened.

"So damn tight." He kissed her. "Perfect," Bennett whispered against her lips.

Then he withdrew. He thrust again. Harder. Rougher. The time for savoring was gone, and she was desperately arching up against him, moving even faster now that her body had adjusted to his. He still had her hands imprisoned, and she tried to yank them down, wanting to touch him.

"I like you this way," he told her. "So beautiful. So mine." He angled his hips so that he pushed down against her core. Her climax was close. She could feel it surging up within her. Closer. Closer.

He thrust. Withdrew. Thrust.

The headboard rammed into the wall. Her legs locked around his hips as she drove up to meet him.

Then her release exploded within her. The pleasure rocked through her body, filling every cell, taking her breath and making her heart race even faster. She tried to say his name, but speech was a little too much for her. She just arched toward him and rode out that climax.

"You feel...*incredible*..." He slid out, then thrust back in. "Squeezing...so *good*..."

Then his hold tightened even more on her wrists. He stiffened against her, then shuddered. Ivy stared up at him, captivated by the pleasure she could see filling his face and blazing in his gaze. He kept thrusting with his release, driving in her again and again, and the slick moves of his body just made her release keep spiraling.

"*Ivy.*"

He kissed her.

She pretty much came apart for him.

In the aftermath, Bennett let her hands go. He brought her wrists to his mouth. Kissed one. Then the other. Did he feel the fast sputter of her pulse beneath his lips?

He slid from her body, and a protest broke from her lips.

"I'll be right back."

He'd better be. She closed her eyes.

She heard the pad of his footsteps but Ivy didn't bother looking to see what he was doing. Her whole body felt limp, languid, pretty damn awesome. She snuggled deeper into the covers and—

Did she hear the sound of running water?

Ivy cracked open one eye. Bennett was back. He bent, slid his arms under her and lifted her up against his chest.

"This is going to stun you," Ivy told him a bit drowsily. "But I can actually walk."

"You just feel so good against me." He carried her toward the bathroom. "I've missed you."

He had a huge, claw-footed tub in the middle of the bathroom. He lowered her into that tub and the warm water was absolute bliss. He stepped in behind her, and they sank down together. The water kept pumping from the brass faucet, filling up the space around them.

Bennett pulled her back against his chest. His hands curled around her stomach and he pressed a kiss to her shoulder.

"I missed you," Bennett said again. She heard the echo of pain in his voice.

"Don't worry," Ivy told him. "I'm not going anywhere." *And this time, neither are you.* They were together now, and nothing would tear them apart again.

***

Cameron Wilde jogged down the beach. He loved the beach at dawn. When the first streaks of the sun's light began to inch across the sky, they always looked so red…like blood. His sneakered feet pounded across the sand, but he made sure to stay out of the waves that reached so greedily toward him. His breath sawed in and out even as his heartbeat pounded steadily.

The sand flew up in his wake. His hands were fisted as he ran and—

Someone was at his beach house. Not just any person, either. A cop car. He saw it from a good mile away. His pace quickened as he hurried forward. A cop shouldn't be visiting his beach house. That was his sanctuary. No one should be there.

But now he could see two uniformed men. One was on his balcony. One was walking down the beach toward him.

"Mr. Wilde!" The cop approaching him yelled.

Cameron waved and kept running. When he was within five feet of that cop, he stopped, his breath heaving. "What's going on?"

"Got orders to check on you, sir." The cop surveyed him, more than a bit suspiciously. "I'm Officer Fred Wayne. The authorities over in Mobile have been trying to reach you."

His gut clenched. Cameron lowered his head, put his hands on his knees, and sucked in a deep breath. "Why? What's happening?" *The authorities...*

Instantly, Ivy's face flashed through his mind.

Oh, hell, no —

"We came by last night, looking for you, sir, but you weren't here."

No, he hadn't been.

"Want to tell us where you were?"

Fucking some girl I met on the beach. A brunette who looked enough like Ivy to get me through the night. But now, he wasn't going to tell the guy that bit. "I was out at one of the bars." True enough. He'd just left the bar after a while.

Fred took another step toward him. "Where is your Porsche, Mr. Wilde?"

Cameron kept his hands on his knees, but he tilted his head back so he could gaze at the cop. "The last time I checked, the Porsche was locked in my garage." He straightened slowly, rolling his shoulders. "I don't bring it here. The sand would just mess up the paint."

The cop frowned.

"I drove the SUV over. It's parked under the cabin, I'm sure you saw it." And the cop was making him nervous. "What's happening?" Cameron demanded again.

"We're going to need you to come with us, sir." Officer Fred glanced over his shoulder. The guy's partner had left the balcony and was walking toward them. Fred cleared his throat and said, "It appears that your Porsche may have been stolen."

"What?" Could he have worse luck?

"It was spotted at the scene of a murder."

Cameron took an aggressive step toward that cop. *"Who was murdered?"* Not Ivy, not—

Fred put his hand on his holster. "Sir, I need you to calm down."

Cameron growled. "I'm wearing a pair of jogging shorts and tennis shoes. I obviously have no weapons, so you're not in any danger from me." He put his hands up, though, so the guys wouldn't get all trigger happy. "Tell me what the hell is going on here."

Fred nervously licked his lips. "You need to go in to the Mobile police station."

Cameron's back teeth ground together.

"A...a Shelly Estes was killed last night, and the perp who killed her, he drove off in *your* car," Fred told him.

Shelly? Cameron shook his head. "No, that's not possible."

"I said too much." Fred backed up a step. "You need to get dressed. They want you in Mobile."

"Shelly?" Cameron whispered. Oh, shit, but Hugh must be a mess. He followed the cop, his steps wooden, his mind whirling.

The killer had used his car? His Porsche? What the hell? It was almost as if… "Is the bastard trying to set me up?" Because cops had come hunting for him, and that shit couldn't be good.

Fred glanced back at him. "You'll probably want your lawyer to meet you in Mobile."

Sonofabitch. "I don't want a lawyer. I want to see my friends." Because Hugh and Ivy would need him.

He would be there for them, no matter what.

CHAPTER TEN

The sunlight poured through the blinds, falling onto the bed. Onto Ivy.

Bennett stared at her, enjoying the way the light caught her hair, bringing out faint red highlights in the dark mane that he had never noticed before.

She was lying face down on the bed, with the sheets pooled around her waist. He stood by the edge of the mattress, and his fingers itched to touch her.

The chief had called him a few minutes ago. The ME wanted to see him — and he was scheduled to meet with the mayor, too. There was no way to keep the murders out of the public eye — hell, by hitting the councilman *and* a high profile society queen like Shelly Estes, the killer had practically guaranteed himself a front page spread in the paper.

A press conference was scheduled for that afternoon.

And, on top of all that, Cameron Wilde had been found — and the guy was due in for an interrogation very soon.

I have to go.

But he just wanted to stay right there, where he knew Ivy was safe. His fingers trailed down her back. "Ivy." He kept his voice soft.

She stretched beneath his touch.

"Ivy..." A little louder now.

Her head turned. Her eyes fluttered open. Her dark gaze focused on him, and she smiled.

When was the last time that someone had looked at him that way? Like he was something good, something...special?

Ivy had always looked at him that way, though. Even when they were teens. When she should have never noticed a guy like him...she'd turned to him and given him that same slow smile.

"I was dreaming about you," Ivy said.

And I've spent most of my life dreaming about you.

She pushed up a bit in the bed. "You were—"

"I have to go back to the station."

Ivy pushed back her hair. She twisted in the bed and brought the sheet up to cover her breasts. A real crying shame.

Bennett cleared his throat. "Cameron Wilde has been found. He's okay," he said quickly when he saw the worry flicker in her gaze. "Seems he was at the beach house, just like you said. He's coming in so I can ask him some questions about the case."

"I'm coming, too," Ivy said immediately.

Yes, he'd thought that would be her response. But he shook his head. "No dice. The chief gave specific instructions that you were *not* to show up." He rubbed a hand over his jaw, feeling the scrape of his stubble. "Everyone knows that you're close with Cameron. The chief said you had to stay away for his interrogation."

"But—"

"And the press are going to be at the station. Chief Quarrel said it was already a feeding frenzy, and the mayor has given orders for us to lock down civilian access as much as possible."

Her head tilted as she stared up at him. "I thought that I was under protective custody."

Her lips were so red. So plump. He leaned down and kissed her. "You are," he said softly. "That's why Detective Drew Trout is outside. He'll be your shadow for today."

Her gaze searched his. "Dumping me isn't cool."

Keeping you safe is.

"You know…I'll just contact Dr. Battiste on my own and find out what he tells you."

Battiste needed to watch his step. If the mayor found out he was sharing details of the investigation, the guy would find himself in some serious hot water.

"Keep close to your guard," Bennett ordered her. "If anything happens to scare you—shit, if

you just feel *nervous,* then call me right away."
And he'd be at her side instantly.

Screw the press conference.

Screw everything...but her.

Her lips lifted into a faint half-smile. "I'm
nervous."

He stilled.

"But that's not how it works. You have a job
to do. So do I. Go." She pushed against his
shoulders. "And come back to me when you
can."

He didn't leave, not yet. "Where are you
planning to go?" Because he could already see
the wheels spinning in her head.

"To see my brother. He'll need me." Her
shoulders rolled back. "Then I'll go pay my
respects to Shelly's family." Her gaze fell to the
covers. "She was my friend, and she deserved so
much better than this." Her breath whispered
out. "So did Evette...so did those other women.
The councilman. No one deserved this
slaughter."

And that was exactly what it had been.

His hand lifted and trailed over her cheek.
"I'll be back at your side before you know it."
She was right—he did have a job to do. Hunting
that psycho out there. And Ivy might want to
hunt right at his side, but he'd tried working
with a partner before...and that man—trained at
the FBI Academy—had fallen to a killer's blade.

Bennett had been trapped with his friend's dead body. The blood had leaked toward him.

That won't ever happen with Ivy. He would never risk her that way.

So, no, she wasn't going with him. He was keeping the guard on her. He was keeping her alive. And he *would* find the bastard hunting in Mobile.

Bennett headed into the den. He grabbed his holster and checked his gun. A quick glance over his shoulder showed him that Ivy had followed him. She stood at the edge of the hallway, with the sheet wrapped around her body.

For an instant, he just stopped. Lost, in her. "Sometimes, I would forget," he heard himself say, "just how beautiful you really were."

Her gaze held his. "I hated what happened. I went to the police, I *told* them that they needed to investigate my father more after that accident. I begged Hugh to talk, but he said…he said he never saw my father take a drop to drink that night. But when my dad hugged me at the scene, I could smell the booze on him." She shook her head. "I am so sorry for what happened to your aunt. To you."

He shook his head. "I never blamed you."

"Didn't you, Bennett?" She pulled the sheet up a bit. "Isn't that why you left?"

He glanced down at the gun in his hand. He put it in the holster. "I left because I was ashamed. My mother…she took your father's money. She took it. She sold her sister's life for fifty thousand dollars."

He heard her sharply indrawn breath. "I didn't know—"

"It wasn't just that..." His breath heaved out. "I went after your father."

"What?"

"I broke into his house." This was a shame he'd carried for too long. Because he'd broken down and given in to his rage. "You weren't there. I had this idea, *this crazy idea*, that I could make him confess. So I went in through the back door. I found the bastard there and he was in his study. Drinking. *Drinking again...*when she was barely cold in the ground." His chin lifted. "I lost it. I attacked him."

She took a step toward him.

She should be backing away.

"Hugh was there. He pulled me off your father. Told me to get the hell away. To stay away—from his father. From you. He said I was the dangerous one." He could still see that scene. His first punch had busted the senator's nose. The man hadn't even tried to fight back. He'd just taken the blows. "I think Hugh was right."

Ivy shook her head.

"I'm the one who attacked. I'm the one who fought. I'm the one who could have gone to jail." His laughter was bitter. "One phone call. That was all it would have taken. Your father came to see me the next day, you see. He made me a deal…get the hell out of town. Or go to jail."

"No!"

"Oh, yeah, he did. But that trip out of town—it came complete with a college education. A ticket to start over, just like the ticket he had given my mother." His breath rushed out as shame burned through him. "And dammit, I took that ticket."

She touched his arm. "You were young, Bennett. You—"

"Didn't want to go to jail? Didn't want to throw my life away? No, I didn't. I gave in to his threats. I took his money—just like my mother did—and I left behind the only thing I really cared about."

Her hand squeezed his arm. "I'm here now." She was.

"We can't change the past," Ivy told him starkly. "I wish to God that we could, but it's over. The most we can do is go forward. Try to make things better."

"Like you did with the Sebastian Jones murder?" He threw that out to see her reaction.

Her expression shut down. "I guess I should have expected you to go dig in my life. Only fair, since I was doing the same thing to yours." Her smile turned bittersweet. "Let me guess…was Dr. Battiste the one who told you about that case?"

Bennett nodded.

"I figured he might do something like that," she murmured. Then she softly sighed and said, "When he learned about the *accident* that my father caused, my grandfather had a stroke. He was in the hospital for months."

And I was gone. I'd left Ivy.

"My grandfather's recovery was slow. He had to learn how to speak again. How to walk. Every moment tore out my heart, and I just wanted to help him." She glanced down at her hands. "So I didn't go away to college. I transferred to a school here. I stayed close to him. I visited him as often as I could, and I tried to give him a reason to fight."

He waited.

"Cold cases." She nodded. "That's what we started with. The cases that the cops weren't trying to solve. I would go in to his room each day. Tell my grandfather about them. Read the files. He had…friends…who were happy to pass those files along to me."

"Friends like the chief?" Bennett murmured. "And Dr. Battiste?"

"He wasn't the chief back then." She turned away. "But yes, like them." The sheet trailed behind her. "My grandfather's body was weak, but his mind was sharp. He hated the way things had become with my family. Once, his investigations business had thrived. It had the best reputation in the southeast." She glanced back at him. "He didn't know that my father had used the employees there to dig up dirt on his competitors so he could win political races. He didn't know that the business he'd built with his blood and his sweat had become a blackmail tool for my dad. We all learned that, too late."

Her father was a real prize.

"As I sat in the hospital room with my grandfather, we made plans to change the business…to get it back to the way it used to be. And we decided we'd just start with two employees." The sheet rustled as she walked. "It was just me and him. And our cold cases. With cold cases, sometimes you just need a fresh pair of eyes."

And he was betting her eyes had been plenty fresh.

"As my grandfather and I poured over the notes, we started to find small clues. Details that others had overlooked. Our first big break came with the Sebastian Jones murder."

Thanks to the tip-off from Dr. Battiste, Bennett had pulled up the original case file for Sebastian Jones. Sebastian had been a sixteen-year-old boy — a boy whose body had been found slumped near a dumpster on the outskirts of the city. Drug paraphernalia had been found on the boy, and he'd been shot in the heart. From all accounts, it had looked like a drug deal gone wrong — with the kid's shooter just vanishing into the night.

Bennett had wanted to dig deeper into the case, but he hadn't been given the time. He waited for Ivy to tell him the rest of the story.

"Sebastian was a straight A student," Ivy said. "His mother told me that he was determined to get a scholarship. He wanted to be a doctor. He wanted to save lives. To change the world. She was adamant that he would *never* be involved with drugs, and the ME's report—"

Ah, that would be her friend Dr. Battiste...

"It showed no drugs in his system. It *did* show gunshot residue on his hands, consistent with him fighting his attacker, trying to wrestle the guy away." Sadness softened her voice. "In the official report, the cops noted that Sebastian's mother had just sent him out to the grocery store. That he had one hundred dollars and that he was supposed to buy a few things on her list." Her voice softened. "We realized he was robbed for that money, and his body was just dropped in that spot—because it was an area well-used by drug dealers. When Sebastian was discovered there, the authorities thought just what the killer wanted..."

"That Sebastian was a drug dealer."

She turned toward him. "So the cops were focusing their efforts on the gangs and the drug trade and they didn't look close to home..." Her smile was bitter. "Home isn't always the safest place, you know. Sometimes, that's where the real monsters live."

He knew just how true that was.

"I went back to Sebastian's home. I interviewed his mother. His step-father. I talked to the neighbors. My grandfather was starting to get better, but it was slow. All so slow...he told me not to go alone, but I had to investigate. For him. For Sebastian." Her breath expelled in a rush. "*For me.* I had to prove that I wasn't going to be like my father. I wasn't going to take an easy way out. I just—*I wasn't.*"

Her hand lifted and she brushed back her hair. "You can't really see the scar now. And it seems almost stupid to show it...considering what you went through."

Scar? She didn't have a scar. He'd touched every inch of her smooth skin.

"Sebastian's step-father kept acting odd. So jittery. His eyes were bloodshot. His answers too fast. No, he hadn't seen Sebastian when he left. Yes, he thought the boy had been trouble— *'always acting so high and mighty when he was no better than me'.* That's what he said but...I thought Sebastian *was* better, way better than the image that guy was presenting to me. So I followed the step-father, acting on a hunch...and *he* was the one doing drugs. The one getting high before he'd go home. And I realized...he was the one who took that hundred dollars from his own step-son, and he left Sebastian to die with the garbage."

He crossed to her. She'd pulled the hair away from the nape of her neck, and now he could see the faint, white line that sliced from just behind her ear around to the back of her head.

What the hell?

"The step-father didn't like being followed, so he turned the tables and he started following *me*. He tracked me to the PI office." Her eyelids lowered. "I didn't realize he had the knife on him. He'd sliced me before I even knew what was happening."

His hand rose to her neck. His fingers traced that scar.

"I hit him, drove at him as hard as I could. He fell back but jumped up and was coming at me again, yelling that he wasn't going to prison because Sebastian had died. He screamed that if Sebastian had just given him the money, the boy wouldn't have died. Sebastian's mistake was that he fought back." Her lashes lifted as her gaze held his. "I fought back, too. I grabbed the lamp from my grandfather's desk, and I threw it at him. Even as it shattered, the office door was flying open. Hugh and Cameron rushed in. They'd heard the guy's confession. He went to jail. Sebastian got his justice."

Yes, he had.

"And I got a new job. One that was scary and hard and so worth every single moment and every drop of sweat and fear. It's a job I intend to keep working, no matter what."

And I thought she wasn't strong enough to handle the dark? I am such a fucking fool.

He bent, and his lips brushed against her scar. He kissed it softly, the same way she'd kissed the marks on his body. "Something you should know," he said. She was naked, sexy as all hell, stronger than steel and… "I love you, Ivy. Sometimes, I think I always have. And I know I always will."

"Bennett?"

He forced himself to step back. "If I get a break in this case, I will be calling you, *partner*."

Her eyes widened.

"Now if I don't get the hell out of here…" His gaze dipped down her sheet-covered body. He swallowed. "I'll be getting you in bed. And as much as I want that — want you — the chief and the mayor are waiting."

He'd said that he loved her. She was pretty much staring at him in shock now. Had she really not known how he felt? Did she truly believe he'd left her before without a second glance? Leaving her had gutted him. For months, he'd walked around like half a person — because he'd left his heart with her.

He never wanted her to doubt how he felt — not ever again. He'd have to show her — every day for the rest of their lives — just how much she truly meant to him.

"I will be calling you," he said again. Then he turned for the door. He'd only taken a few steps when Ivy said—

"Don't you want to know how I feel?"

He glanced back. "I'm scared to know," he said starkly. And that was the truth. He'd screwed things up between them. But if she would just give him time, he could build her trust back. Maybe even get her to care for him again.

"Oh, Bennett...you should never be afraid, not with me." Her smile was tender. "I loved you since I was eighteen. It's not the same love now, but I have a feeling that it's going to be even better than before."

Stay with her. He wanted to, so badly. He wanted to stay and hold her and never let go.

But a killer was out there. One who threatened Ivy. One who had to be stopped.

"Partners, huh?" Ivy smiled and his heart stopped at that beautiful sight. "I really like that."

So did he.

She headed back down the hallway. He didn't move, not until she was gone, then, his steps wooden, he exited the house.

She loves me. She still loves me.

He was such a lucky bastard.

"Morning, Bennett!" Detective Drew Trout called out. The guy hurried up the sidewalk, giving him a quick nod.

Bennett stepped directly into the man's path. He and the chief had decided that Drew would be the best person to keep watch over Ivy while Bennett was gone. The young detective was smart, tough, and he should be able to handle any threat that came up.

But...Bennett's voice was curt as he said, "You stay with her, every moment. You keep your eyes on her. If *anything* happens that makes you even a little bit nervous, you call me, right away, got it?"

Drew's Adam's apple bobbed. "Yes, sir. You know, this isn't my first time working a case."

Yeah, he knew, and that was why Bennett had picked the fellow. He didn't trust any of the uniforms with a case of this magnitude. *I don't really trust anyone with Ivy.* Bennett's eyes narrowed. "She *is* the priority in this case, got it? You don't jeopardize her for any reason."
Because if you do, I will kick your ass.

"Sir." Drew nodded quickly.

Good. They'd better be clear. Bennett hurried to his car. He climbed inside, cranked the engine, but didn't leave. His gaze slid to his house once more.
She said...she loves me.

His fingers drummed against the wheel.

He hated the case right then. He hated anything that was keeping him away from Ivy.

CHAPTER ELEVEN

"I'm telling you," Cameron Wilde said as he paced in the interrogation room at the Mobile police station. "I don't know where the Porsche is." His hands fisted as he snarled, "It's supposed to have one of those fancy security systems! You know, the kind where you can just ping some shit and the car is instantly located in the case of theft." He stopped pacing and shot Bennett a furious glare. "I paid too much damn money for the car to just be gone!"

Bennett lifted a brow. "You were told by the Fort Morgan officers that the car was linked to a murder."

Cameron paled. "Yes. Shelly. Poor, sweet Shelly..." He marched to the little table in the middle of the room and pulled out the chair across from Bennett. Cameron sat down, his body falling a bit heavily. "I tried to call Hugh on my way here, but he didn't answer. Shit, I hope he doesn't wind up like his old man. Is the guy on suicide watch?"

Bennett didn't let his expression alter. "Ivy was going to be with him." He'd had the same fears about Hugh, especially after last night.

"So messed up." Cameron's head sagged forward. "None of this was supposed to happen."

That was an odd turn of phrase. A bit wary now, Bennett studied the other man. "Just what *was* supposed to happen?"

Cameron's shoulders stiffened. Very slowly, he glanced up. "Hugh was supposed to marry Shelly."

Bennett reached for the manila file on his left. He wanted to see Cameron's reaction to the photo. "I guess when Shelly changed her hair color, she was too much of a temptation for the killer."

"She...changed her hair color?"

He flipped open the file and pushed a crime scene photo toward Cameron.

The guy's eyelids barely twitched. "She's a brunette now."

She was also covered in blood. She was your friend. And you're just staring at her with almost clinical curiosity.

"Stabbed, like the others?" Cameron asked.

"Others?" Bennett cocked his head to the side.

Cameron flushed. "Look, stop it. Stop trying to jerk me around. You think I haven't been following this case? The minute Ivy was involved, I got involved, too."

Had he?

"Others...*others*," Cameron snapped. "The councilman, that woman at the parade—Evette something or other."

"Evette Summers" Bennett supplied, still watching the other man carefully.

"Right. Evette Summers." Cameron cleared his throat. "How damn tragic."

Bennett's instincts were on full alert. He'd never liked Cameron, mostly because the guy had always been sniffing around Ivy.

"It's actually even more tragic than we first assumed." Bennett pulled the photo away. He noticed that Cameron's gaze followed the image until it was placed back in the folder. "There are more victims."

"More?"

"Quite a few more," he said casually. "Here...and in New Orleans."

Cameron leaned forward. "Are you serious?"

"Dead serious."

"Just how long has this madman been killing? And why hasn't he been stopped?" Cameron jumped to his feet. "Shelly is gone, murdered...and this animal is still out on the streets?"

"For the moment." He looked up at Cameron. The guy had taken up a dominant position, towering over him. *Why would he feel the need to claim dominance?* Bennett had learned a whole lot regarding body language when he'd been hunting with the Violent Crimes division at the FBI.

"You can be assured," Bennett continued slowly as he rose and faced off against Cameron, "that I will not rest until this perp is apprehended."

"This *perp*." There was the faintest emphasis on that last word. "Good. Good. I hope you catch him and you kill him." Cameron whirled on his heel and marched for the door.

I never said we were done. "Killing him isn't my goal. Arresting him is."

Cameron's hand was almost touching the door, but he stopped and looked back at Bennett. "They *look* like Ivy," he rasped. "I see it, and I know you see it, too. That Evette — her picture was splashed in the paper. I thought she *was* Ivy at first. And now Shelly is killed — killed when her hair goes dark like Ivy's…" He yanked a hand over his face. "The killer — the *perp* — is going to come for Ivy. While you're in here, showing me pictures of — *Shelly was my friend!*" He suddenly exploded. "She shouldn't have died!" He gulped in a deep gasp of air. "But Ivy…Ivy could be next."

Bennett stalked toward him. "Just how do you feel about Ivy DuLane?"

Cameron laughed, but the sound was bitter. "How do you *think* I feel? I've been in love with her my whole damn life. Hung up on a girl who could never see past you, not even when you left her. When you took her father's money and roared out of town and didn't so much as glance back to see that you'd *wrecked* her."

Ivy wasn't wrecked. She was strong. Determined. Smart.

"I stayed by her. I stayed by Hugh. Their father only lasted a year before the guilt ate him up and he put that gun in his mouth." His eyes glittered. "You think that shit was easy? She mourned without you. All that time — without you."

"You know I came back then," Bennett bit out the words. He had come back, so desperate for her. But when he'd gotten to the DuLane home, Cameron had met him at the door. "You're the one who told me — "

"That Ivy had moved on." A mocking smile curled Cameron's lips. "Because I thought that she really might. I thought she'd finally give me my chance. But it didn't work. She could *never* see past you. Even though you're the worst thing that could ever happen to her."

The sonofabitch had lied to him. "You never told Ivy I was there, did you?"

Cameron glared at him.

Bennett wanted to drive his fist into Cameron's jaw.

"I would have been good to her," Cameron said, voice rough. "I thought that night we were together, she'd see…"

Bennett's hands had fisted.

"But the next morning, she would barely look at me." Cameron's jaw jutted up. "Is that what you want to hear? That I was desperate for her and she couldn't stand the sight of me…because I wasn't you?"

"I love her," Bennett said flatly.

Rage flashed in Cameron's gold stare. "Why does she love you back? *Why you?*" Then Cameron shook his head in disgust. "You should have done us all a favor and just let the Greenville Trapper kill your ass."

Now Bennett fully understood. Cameron hated him. Good to know. *I hate his skinny ass, too.*

"I'm done here, Detective. You have more questions for me, then you talk to my lawyer. Right now, my friends need me. The friends *I* never abandoned." He threw another look of disgust at Bennett and then stomped from the room.

Bennett picked up the manila file and headed back into the bullpen. He saw that Cameron had stopped and was talking animatedly with the chief. Probably making threats. *Against me, no doubt.*

Then Cameron stormed toward the exit doors.

Bennett approached the chief.

The chief whistled. "Someone sure is pissed off."

Bennett gazed after the guy. "I don't trust that guy."

"Is it personal, though, Detective? Or professional?"

"Personally, I want to beat the hell out of him, sir." Bennett's fingers tightened around the file. "And professionally...something is wrong. During that whole interview, his affect was off."

The chief cleared his throat. "Uh, yeah, he just found out that his friend was murdered. That the killer stole *his* car and fled the murder scene. The man could be in shock."

Could be... "I want to dig deeper into his life." A hell of a lot deeper.

The chief raised a brow. "And this has nothing to do with the fact that the papers have been linking him and Ivy DuLane for years?"

Was he jealous of the guy? Hell, yes, he was jealous of any man who'd gotten too close to Ivy. They'd slept together. And that made him see damn blazing red. But...

But it *wasn't* just personal. "I want to dig deeper," Bennett said flatly. Because something was off. Just wrong.

The chief slapped his hand down on Bennett's shoulder. "Then go get a big shovel. Do whatever the hell you need to do." He brought his head in close to Bennett. "Just find out what's happening in my city."

He would. And he knew where he wanted to start. "Let's put a tail on Cameron Wilde..."

***

"Hugh?" Ivy called as she opened the door to her brother's condo. She always kept a key, for emergencies and those too frequent times when her brother went out for a jog and accidentally locked himself out. He lived just a few blocks from her place, so she'd spent plenty of days running over to help him.

Today wasn't one of those lost key days.

Today...

"*Miss?*" Detective Trout reached for her wrist. The light glinted off his blond hair. "Why don't you let me go in first?"

Hugh hadn't answered when she'd knocked on the door. Or when she'd called him, again and again. So she'd let herself in. And she could tell by the worry on the cop's face that he didn't think they were going to find a good scene inside that condo.

Everyone knows my father killed himself. That was his legacy.

It wouldn't be Hugh's. "My brother is okay," she said fiercely.

"Let me go in first." Now the cop's voice was firm.

Ivy stepped back. Her heart was pounding too fast. Her hands were shaking and they just wouldn't stop. The cop drew his gun and slowly entered the condo.

Hugh, don't do this. Don't do this, please!

"Hugh DuLane!" Detective Trout yelled. "I'm with the Mobile PD. Your sister is here —"

There was a groan. A pain-filled sound that tore at Ivy's chest. She leapt forward, trying to push around the cop.

He pushed her back. "Hugh DuLane!" The detective's voice was a yell.

Ivy got a good look at the inside of the condo. The place was trashed. Glass shattered. Couch cushions overturned. The TV had been thrown against a wall.

Her hand rose, covering her mouth.

"Leave...." A low snarl.

Her gaze jerked to the left. Hugh was there, standing. Staggering, really. He lifted a hand and put it to the wall for support. "Just...leave."

No, she wasn't leaving him. Dodging the cop, Ivy ran to her brother's side. "Hugh..." She could smell the alcohol wafting off him. "What did you do to yourself?"

His bleary eyes blinked at her. "I only left her for a few minutes, Ives. Just a few minutes..."

She wrapped her hands around him and held on tight.

"Just like with dad…I only left him for a few minutes…and then I heard the boom…"

***

"We've got a team on Cameron Wilde," Chief Quarrel said as he strode into Bennett's office. "Just like you asked. Hell, I figured it couldn't be a bad thing. The guy should even thank us. I mean, the killer stole his car. Could mean he's next on the victim list."

"Our killer was just supposed to like women with dark hair," Bennett said as he tried to reason out this damn case. "If he's a true serial…hunting to quench some desire that he feels…or a rage that's directed at a woman who physically looks that way…then why the hell is the councilman dead? Shouldn't the killer have hesitated a bit? I mean, if he only goes after women, then he seriously changed up his pattern."

"Not if it was just a crime of opportunity," the chief argued. "That's what he pretty much told you when he called Ivy, right? That the councilman got in his way…"

And I can't help but wonder…has anyone else ever gotten in the killer's way? Bennett's fingers flew over the keyboard. And finally — finally — he got access to the records that he needed. His gaze scanned over the notes from the first officer on scene.

"Uh, Detective Morgan?"

"He was the one who found the body," Bennett said as he quickly scanned the material on the screen.

"Excuse me?" The chief advanced and the floor creaked beneath his feet.

Bennett didn't spare him a glance. "According to this report, when Senator DuLane committed suicide, two other people were in the house—his son Hugh and Hugh's best friend, Cameron Wilde."

He put a gun in his mouth. Cameron had said those words so coldly.

"The way he talked when I had him in interrogation, I suspected that Cameron had found the body, and he did." It was right there in the report. Hugh had gone out for a swim. And Cameron had been the one inside the house. He'd been the one to rush into the Senator's bedroom and find him sprawled on the ground.

"The senator's case?" Now the chief was leaning over him to stare at the screen, too. "Why are you digging that back up now? Is it because of what Hugh said last night?"

"Not Hugh." *He was outside.* "Cameron Wilde." He clicked the mouse and opened photos taken from the scene of the senator's death. "Look, he had blood on his clothes..." He saw the clothes right there. Pictures of them. They'd been bagged and tagged for evidence.

His eyes narrowed as he read about that analysis.

"Well, yes, of course there was blood on him." The chief sounded aggrieved now. "He tried to revive the guy at first. That's what he told the officers. You think I don't remember this case? It's not every day a man like DuLane eats his gun."

Did he eat it?

"Although why the hell Cameron tried to revive him is beyond me," Chief Quarrel said gruffly. "The senator was missing half of his damn head."

That picture was there, too. Horrifying. Gory. A picture of the senator...with the gun still cradled in his hand.

Only...*Is that right? If he'd fired the gun, wouldn't it have fallen from his fingers when the bullet slammed into his head? At impact, he should have lost control of his hand, not continued gripping the weapon, even in death.*

At the very least, when the senator fell to the floor, the gun should have flown from his hand. Not still been held so conveniently there.

Bennett tapped on the keyboard again and went right back to reading the report about Cameron's blood stained clothes and—"Gunshot residue."

"Dammit, man, focus on *this* case!" The chief snarled, his patience obviously gone. "We don't need to waste time in the past just because some—"

Bennett whirled his chair toward him. "Ivy said that sometimes cold cases just need a fresh pair of eyes."

"That sounds like her," the chief muttered.

Bennett pulled up the picture of the senator's body. "The gun *shouldn't* still be in his hand." The odds of that—*too low*. "And why was gunshot residue on Cameron's shirt?"

"He…he might have just brushed against the weapon. Or against the senator's hand or—"

"Or maybe *he* fired the weapon."

The chief stepped back. "You're saying Cameron Wilde killed the senator?"

Bennett surged to his feet. "It was the way he acted in interrogation. All wrong. Just…too cold. He didn't even flinch when he saw the picture of Shelly's body."

"Having a strong stomach doesn't make a man a killer!"

No, but having gunshot residue on his clothes…being in the same house with the senator…being—

"Everyone knew the senator was spiraling out of control." Chief Quarrel's voice was even rougher now. "His suicide was no surprise. I would think you, of all people, would have been glad that justice was served."

It hadn't been justice. Not even close. "Everyone thought he killed himself…so no one looked deep enough into the case."

Not even Ivy? Or her grandfather? But maybe…maybe her father's death had hurt her too much. His life and his death. So she had worked other cases, but never his.

"You got the number for the officers who are trailing Wilde?" Bennett demanded. The guy had been gone about thirty minutes — and Bennett needed to know just where the fellow was at that moment.

"Officers Brady and Givens." The chief immediately rattled off Brady's number. Bennett yanked out his phone and called the officer. The line rang once, twice.

"Officer Brady."

"You still have eyes on Wilde?"

"Yes, sir…he's just…he went back to his house. He's gone inside and pulled the blinds shut. His car is out front."

"If he leaves, if he moves at all, you call me right away, got it?"

Because he didn't trust Wilde. And it wasn't just about Ivy and the past they shared. It was something deeper. Darker.

***

"When I heard that shot, I jumped out of the pool and ran inside as fast as I could," Hugh said, his voice halting. "I was dripping water everywhere and I thought about how much Dad would hate that. You know how he always wanted the house to look perfect. The perfect house to hide our screwed up family."

She squeezed him harder.

"Cameron was in Dad's room. When I ran in, he was standing over Dad. Staring at him. I didn't even understand what the hell had happened, not until Cameron looked up and told me...he said it was all over now. Dad had killed himself."

He shuddered against her.

"That's what one of the cops told me last night," Hugh whispered. "Same stupid words. That Shelly was *gone*. That it was all over for her. *All over.* What the hell does that even mean?"

She looked up at him. "How much have you had to drink?"

"Not enough. I can still see Shelly. I see her everywhere."

She glanced around the wrecked house. "Is that why you've been breaking everything?"

"Ives...I'm scared. I don't think I can do this without her."

"*Hugh.*" She snapped out his name, saying it hard and fast.

His bleary stare met hers.

"You can do this. You *will* do this, do you understand me? You aren't going out like our father. You are going to get through this.

Because I'm going to be with you. We always stick together, don't we? No matter what?"

Hugh nodded.

"We're going to find the man who hurt Shelly. We're going to stop him."

His shoulders straightened a bit.

"You have to get yourself together, though, Hugh. You have to get some sleep. Eat. Stop drinking." *Don't take our father's path.*

"It hurts…"

"I know. And it's probably going to hurt a lot more before it gets better." She wouldn't lie to him. The funeral would be hell. "But doesn't Shelly deserve justice? Don't you want to give her that?"

"*Yes.*"

Damn straight. "Good. Then let's get you to bed and—"

"I…wrecked the bed."

She frowned at him, then went to investigate. She peeked in the room and sure enough—"Why?" She turned around and Hugh was behind her. The detective had waited in the den.

"Because the sheets smelled of her. Because I could still feel her there."

Ivy nodded. "Okay, then we're going back to my place." Because she wasn't leaving her brother alone. "You'll stay in my guest room. And we'll get through this—together." She offered her hand to him.

He stared at her fingers. Slowly, his hand rose and curled around hers. "Is this what it felt like for you?"

"What do you mean?"

"When Bennett left you? Is this what it was like? You hated the whole damn world and pain was ripping your guts out?"

She'd hurt, so much, but it wasn't the same. Bennett had still been alive. Just not with her. Shelly… "Everything is going to be all right." But those words felt like such a lie.

And his bitter smiled called her on that lie. "I told him to leave you. To never look back. I saw what he did to Dad. Saw the way he attacked him…he was dangerous, Ivy. I thought he'd hurt you."

"Let's go, Hugh."

"But I'm the one who hurt you…I forced him to leave, threatened him with jail. *I* did that to you. Not just Dad, me." His fingers squeezed hers. "I'm so sorry."

So was she. For so many things. *Bennett never mentioned that Hugh threatened him. Just my father.*

Why had he kept that part secret?

Hugh didn't speak again as they left his condo. Their guard watched them, the detective's face grim. At least the guy hadn't needed to use his gun. Her brother was safe.

She'd make sure he stayed that way.

***

Bennett's phone rang just as he was heading out to his car. He yanked the phone to his ear. "Bennett."

"Detective Morgan? He's...he's gone sir."

"Officer Brady?"

"I got worried because his place was so quiet. I went to the door, knocked — "

So much for keeping a low profile.

"The house is empty. The back door was unlocked, so I-I searched the place before calling you."

Sonofabitch.

"He's gone." The cop sounded miserable. "He must have left on foot."

"Start searching the area. Maybe he just went out for a damn jog or something." The cops from Fort Morgan had said they'd found Cameron jogging on the beach. "Look for him. *Find* him. Call in extra units." Because he was afraid it wasn't going to be something as simple as a run.

He was afraid...afraid that Cameron's obsession with Ivy might have grown too much over the years. Grown so much that he started seeking out women with long, dark hair, just like hers. Women who were close to Ivy's age.

Women he'd killed.

Because Ivy had rejected him?

"Find him," Bennett ordered flatly. "Find. Him."

CHAPTER TWELVE

Ivy turned off the alarm at her house. She cast a nervous smile toward Detective Trout. She felt so bad having the guy trail her. He was a detective, for goodness sake. He probably wanted to be out, hitting the streets, looking for clues. *Not playing guard duty.* "Why don't you relax in the den, Detective?" she offered. "I'm going to get my brother settled in upstairs."

"You need some help?" the detective asked.

"No, but thank you." She steered Hugh toward the stairs. "Feel free to grab a bite from the kitchen. Or if you want to run out and get something…I mean, I'm safe here. And I'm not alone."

"She's got me," Hugh mumbled.

But the detective shook his head. "My orders were to stay close." But his gaze slid toward the kitchen. "Though I could go for a sandwich."

"Help yourself." She flashed him a nervous smile, then turned back to her brother. He was wavering on his feet. They climbed the stairs together, then she turned to the right, heading for the guest room.

Her brother pretty much fell into the bed. He put his hand over his eyes. "I hope I dream about her," he muttered. "Then maybe...maybe I can pretend she's still with me."

She pulled the covers over him.

"Love you, Ives..."

"And I love you." She shut the blinds, darkening the room. She slipped back into the hallway and shut the door behind her. Ivy dug her phone out of her pocket. She should call Bennett and tell him that she'd gone back home. Maybe he could update her on the case. Tell her what was happening.

She put the phone to her ear.

***

Ivy was back. She'd finally returned home. Only...

She wasn't alone. He'd heard the voices. The footsteps.

Her brother. A cop.

Too many eyes. Too many distractions.

Did she think they'd keep her safe? They weren't going to stop him. No one was going to stop him. Ivy was his key. No, his mirror. She saw beneath his mask.

He'd do anything for her.

Now he knew why she mattered so much. It was all clear to him.

He stood in her pantry, waiting. He'd been in that house for so long, just waiting for her to come back. A knife was gripped in his left hand, and he had his mask on.

Waiting…

Hugh had been so stupid to keep the security code for Ivy's house on his phone. Such a dumb mistake. But then, Hugh wasn't the brightest fellow. So blind. So easily misled.

He'd known she would be back to her home, sooner or later.

Footsteps padded closer to him. He'd left the pantry door cracked open, just a bit, and he saw the cop approaching. He backed up a bit, heading into the darkness of that pantry. The shadows.

Come and get me…

The pantry door opened.

A blond man stood there. Had to be the one Ivy had called "detective". Behind his mask, the killer smiled. The cop wasn't even looking at him. He was staring at the bread on the nearby shelf. The guy strolled inside as if he owned the place.

You don't.

The cop reached for the bread.

The killer gripped the weapon in his hand — and he stabbed the bastard with his knife.

The cop opened his mouth to scream. *Can't have that.* Before that sound could escape, the killer clamped his left hand over the guy's lips. He stabbed the cop again and again.

He stabbed him until the man's body stopped twitching.

Until the detective just slid to the floor.

***

"Bennett? Hi...um, I'm home," Ivy said when he answered her call. She paused near her bedroom door.

"*Ivy.*"

She liked the way he said her name. Liked the need and the—

"Is the detective still with you?" Bennett demanded.

She smiled. "He's downstairs. Don't worry. I'm totally safe." She strolled into her room. Gazed down at the street below. It was broad daylight, and the moss hanging from the oak tree at the end of her drive swayed lightly in the breeze. "Hugh is with me, too. Though he's currently sleeping like—" *The dead.* She cleared her throat. "He's sleeping." She paced back toward the bedroom door. "Bennett, did you learn anything new? Did you—"

Her doorbell rang.

Ivy paused. She'd just looked out the window. There had been no cars in front of her house. She hadn't seen anyone walking in the street.

"What's wrong?" Bennett asked her.

"Nothing. Someone's just at the door."

She hurried from her room, keeping the phone pressed to her ear as she headed down the stairs. "Hugh just got to sleep. I don't want anyone to wake him up." She rushed past the kitchen. From the corner of her eye, she saw the detective, standing just inside her pantry. "I have to get the door," Ivy told Bennett. "Give me just a second…"

She peeked through her curtains, trying to get a glimpse of her porch. She couldn't see anyone though and —

The doorbell rang again.

"Get Detective Trout to check outside." Bennett's voice sounded angry. "Don't open the door."

She took a step away from the window. "Okay. Just settle down, all right? You're making *me* nervous." She cleared her throat. *And I'm already plenty nervous enough.* He didn't have to help the situation any.

"*Ivy!*" The doorbell rang again, right after that loud cry, and she jumped. "It's Cameron!"

Her breath expelled in a quick rush. "It's okay, Bennett," she told him quickly. "I know who's at the door."

The floor creaked behind her. She didn't look back. Detective Trout must be heading her way.

"Cameron's at the door," Ivy said to Bennett, "I'll call you right back —"

"No!" Now his voice sounded desperate.

Ivy had just started to reach for the doorknob with her left hand. Her fingers stilled.

"Don't let him in. Don't open the door. I think he's a killer, Ivy."

What?

The floor squeaked behind her once more.

"I think he killed —"

The door shook beneath what had to be Cameron's pounding fists. "Ivy!" He bellowed. "Let me in!"

She spun around, thinking the detective must have been behind her — she'd heard his footsteps, right? Or at least, the creak of the floor beneath him.

But…no one was there.

"Who do you think he killed?" Ivy asked Bennett. Then she laughed because this was crazy. Cameron was her friend, not a killer. "Not Shelly. And he…he doesn't even have the right hair color, Bennett. I told you, that night at the Order of Pharaohs ball, the man in the mask had dark hair. Cameron has blond hair."

The door had stopped shaking beneath Cameron's fists.

"Ivy, get Detective Trout," Bennett said grimly.

That was what she was *trying* to do! She hurried to the kitchen. The pantry door was still slightly ajar. "Who do you think Cameron killed?" Ivy demanded again.

"Your father."

She almost dropped the phone. That was just...just crazy. No way had Cameron killed her father. Her father had committed suicide. Her fingers—quivering just a bit—reached for the pantry door. She opened it.

It was dark inside.

Ivy flipped the light switch.

And saw the body on the floor.

"Ivy, Ivy talk to me..."

She rushed inside and nearly slipped in the blood. So much blood. "Bennett..." She put her hand to the detective's throat. "He's dead, Bennett. Detective Trout is dead."

"Cameron is in the house!"

"No." Her voice had dropped to a whisper. "He's at the front door. Detective Trout is dead inside. The killer is *inside*." A killer that *wasn't* Cameron.

Then, up above her, she heard a creak. Ivy's head tipped back as she stared at the ceiling. Her guest room was directly above the pantry. Hugh was up there. Asleep.

Helpless.

And I don't think he is alone.

"Hurry, Bennett. *Hurry.*" She shot out of the pantry. "Because I can't let him kill my brother!"

"Ivy, Ivy, baby, no, whatever—"

"I love you," she whispered. Then Ivy shoved the phone into her back pocket because she couldn't keep the phone in her grasp when she was fighting that jerk upstairs. She spun around in her kitchen, looking for a weapon.

She had a block of knives on her counter, and she grabbed the butcher knife.

Then she ran for the stairs.

***

"Ivy? *Ivy!*" Bennett yelled.

But there was no answer.

Shit, shit, shit! He floored the gas even as he put in a frantic call to the PD. He gave the dispatcher Ivy's address and told her, "An officer is down and the suspected perp is *in* the house." In the house—Dear God, with Ivy. "Get units there, now!"

But he would get there before they arrived. He was just a few miles away.

Just a few…

But Ivy had never seemed farther from him.

I love you. Her last words whispered through his mind, driving him right to the edge of sanity. If he got there and Ivy was hurt…if she was lying dead in a pool of blood, like Shelly…

No, baby, no.

He raced right through a red light, honking his horn to alert the other drivers. Fear was an acid, burning in his gut. Ivy—she was all he could think about. Ivy was the only thing that mattered.

Ivy. He prayed that he wouldn't get to her...too late.

***

Ivy wasn't letting him in.

Cameron backed away from her front door. He was lucky the neighbors hadn't already called the cops on him. But he'd been forced to yell and pound at Ivy's door so she'd know it was him out there. He hadn't brought his phone with him when he'd ditched those cops who'd been on his trail. He'd needed her to know it was him on her porch. Needed her to understand that she was safe.

After their little chat at the station, it had been abundantly clear that Bennett suspected him. The guy's green gaze had glittered with fury as he stared at Cameron. So who knew what shit the detective had told Ivy? He had to reassure her.

Only Ivy still hadn't answered the door.

Because she believed Bennett's lies or...

He jumped off her porch and stared up at the house. Ivy's room was to the left. And the guest room was to the right. The blinds were drawn in the guest room.

He looked back over his shoulder. A sedan was at the end of the street. It looked like an unmarked police car to him. But…if it was…if Ivy was in the house with a cop…

She would have answered the door.

Ivy was his friend. There was only one reason she wouldn't let him in.

Because she's in trouble.

Dammit, Ivy needed him.

He ran around to the back of the house. Her back door was made partially of glass. The front door was too hard to break through, but the back—*I'll bust my way inside.*

Because he *was* getting to Ivy.

***

Ivy rushed off the stairs. She flew toward the guest room.

And she nearly ran into the man who was waiting for her. A tall man, with broad shoulders. A man wearing a white Mardi Gras mask that totally covered his face. The mask covered everything, except his bright blue eyes.

She looked into those eyes…and saw evil staring back at her.

She jumped away from him and lifted her knife. "Who the hell are you?"

His eyes gleamed. "The man in the mask…"

He was just a few feet away from Hugh's door. And there was…there was a bloody knife in his hand.

Her lips trembled. "What did you do?"

"I made sure we could be alone." He made no move toward her. Just held his knife.

She held hers.

"Mirror, mirror…pretty broken mirror…" he whispered.

She inched down the hallway. "Hugh?" His name emerged as a broken cry. She tried again. Louder. "Hugh?"

The man in the mask laughed. "He can't answer…"

Her fingers tightened around her butcher knife.

"Such a shame…"

He'd said that before. In that dark corridor at the Order of Pharaohs ball.

Inside, Ivy was breaking apart. Breath by breath. Her heart was splintering. But she tried her best not to show any fear. She suspected he'd like her fear too much. "The police are coming."

His bright blue gaze darted to her knife. "Think you'll kill me before they get here?"

Yes. Because if he'd stabbed her brother, if he'd taken Hugh from her, *I will kill him.*

"I'm not the one you should fear, sweet Ivy. It was never *my* plan."

Glass shattered. The sharp sound came from downstairs and Ivy jerked. Her gaze flew toward the stairs.

And the man in the mask lunged toward her.

"No!" Ivy lifted her knife and she drove it into his stomach. There was a sickening, wet sound as that blade cut deep and his blue eyes widened.

"Ivy…" Anger and pain twisted in his voice. Her knife was still in his stomach.

And *his* knife was at her throat. She remembered another time. Another knife. Sebastian Jones's step-father had wanted to cut her throat, too.

But she'd held him off.

Then Hugh and Cameron had arrived…

"Ivy!"

Relief nearly made her dizzy. That was Cameron's voice. Cameron pounded up the stairs. Her alarm was shrieking, and she knew that he must have broken in through her back door. *That* shattering she'd heard had been the door's glass panel breaking.

"If you move," the man in the mask told her, "I will cut you ear to ear."

She had her knife buried to the hilt in him but he was still standing there, like some terrible movie monster, far too strong.

"Ivy…" Cameron sounded so close. So desperate.

Her gaze slid toward him. He was right at the landing, and his gaze glittered wildly.

"The police are coming," she managed to say, choking back her fear. "He's not going to get away."

Cameron shook his head. "No. He won't. I promise you that."

Cameron was wearing jogging shorts and a t-shirt. His body was covered in a light film of sweat, as if he'd run to her house.

"I know a secret," the man in the mask said to Ivy, his voice nearly gloating. "Want to hear it?"

Then he leaned in real close to her.

Her fingers were slick around the handle of her butcher knife, slick with his blood and her sweat.

The masked man's lips feathered over her ear. "You're not safe..."

That wasn't a secret. He had a damn knife at her throat. Ivy tensed, knowing what she had to do. She'd need to move fast. She'd have to hit him again, take him *down*.

Or I'll die...

"He's the one who wants you," the masked man rasped. "He's the one who started it all..."

What?

"Your *friend*...Cameron..."

Once more, her gaze cut to Cameron. He was advancing, slowly and...Cameron had a knife in his hand. She could just see it — hidden behind his leg. Another one of her kitchen knives.

"*He did it all...*" The masked man told her. "And you never knew."

Ivy yanked back on the handle of her knife. There was a wet *slosh* as the blade slid out of her attacker.

His knife sliced over her neck and —

Cameron roared. He attacked. Cameron grabbed the masked man and yanked him away from Ivy. Then he drove his knife right at the killer's chest.

Only the masked man seemed far too ready for his attack. He dodged that blade and launched himself at Cameron. Their bodies twisted — Cameron and that masked man — and they fell back, tumbling down the stairs again and again with a sickening crunch of bones.

And then they stopped, a heap at the bottom of the stairs. Ivy stared down at them, horrified.

The masked man began to move.

So did Cameron. Cameron drove his fist at the other guy.

She looked at the bloody knife in her hand, and Ivy crept down the stairs.

CHAPTER THIRTEEN

Bennett slammed on the brakes and jumped out of his car. The car door hung open as he raced toward Ivy's house. He grabbed for that front doorknob, but it was locked. "Ivy!" The door was hard, sturdy, reinforced…and there was going to be no breaking it in easily.

But the back door isn't like this one. He remembered seeing it before — and thinking that Ivy needed more security back there.

He ran to the back door and saw the broken glass littering the ground. The door was open, swaying a bit in the breeze. He rushed inside. "*Ivy!*" He had to find her.

Then he heard the grunts, the thud of fists hitting flesh.

Bennett burst out of the kitchen. Two men were fighting at the foot of the stairs. Cameron Wilde and a man with dark hair, a man bleeding and snarling.

A white Mardi Gras mask lay just a few feet from the struggling men.

Ivy was there, inching down the stairs. Her gaze was totally locked on the two men. The knife in her hand dripped blood and she began to lift it. Up, up—

He had his gun out and he aimed it at the two men. "Freeze the fuck *now!*"

They froze. Cameron jerked away from the man and his desperate gaze found Bennett. "Shoot him, now! He came to kill Ivy!"

The alarm blared all around them. Bennett caught sight of a white Mardi Gras mask on the floor—part of the mask had broken away. "I said freeze," Bennett roared. "Both of you!"

Ivy was on the steps, far too close to those damn men. His gaze flew over them—Cameron had blood dripping from his busted lip. The other man—he was just as Ivy had described the first night. Tall, broad-shouldered, dark-haired. His blue eyes glittered and a smirk twisted his lips.

Both men appeared unarmed.

Appeared.

Both men were also between him and Ivy, and that shit just wasn't going to fly.

"The place is going to be swarming with cops in moments." Bennett motioned to the dark-haired man. "You're not getting away."

The man laughed.

"*Shoot* him!" Cameron yelled. "He killed Shelly, he killed—"

"My brother," Ivy said, her voice breaking.

Oh, fuck. Bennett didn't even know how Ivy was holding things together if Hugh was dead.

"Hugh?" Cameron shook his head. "Not Hugh. He's...he's my best friend." And he sounded confused.

The dark-haired man laughed. "And that's how your fucking house of cards goes down...*down, down, down...*"

Bennett knew Cameron was going to attack. He saw the man's eyes blaze with hate and rage and—

Cameron lunged for the killer. Only the killer was moving, too. But not going toward Cameron. The man turned and grabbed for Ivy.

She slashed out with the knife, and it cut across the killer's forearm. The man yelled and he reached for her again. She sliced out with a butcher knife once more.

Cameron drove his fist into the man's back. "She was never for you! Leave her the hell alone!"

The dark-haired man rammed his elbow into Cameron's face. Bones crunched and Cameron fell back, howling in pain.

Bennett was already racing forward. He jumped over Cameron, intent on his target. Before that bastard could grab for Ivy again, Bennett had his gun pressed to the back of the man's head. "I told you to freeze before. Move again, so much as an inch, and I will pull the trigger."

Cameron was behind him, still moaning and groaning, but from the sound of things, getting to his feet.

Ivy stood just two steps above the killer. The knife was clenched in her fist. Her eyes burned with her fear and horror.

He killed Hugh.

The man in front of Bennett...laughed.

Bennett's finger started to squeeze that trigger.

"This is almost like the way your father went out," the man murmured to Ivy. "Isn't it? Except the gun is at the back of my head, not being forced *into* my mouth by Cameron."

Ivy's face bleached of its last remaining bit of color. She lifted the knife, as if she'd stab the man again.

"Don't, Ivy," Bennett said because...shit, hadn't he suspected the same thing? That Cameron had killed Ivy's father? But how — how did the man in front of him know that?

That's how your fucking house of cards goes down, down, down...

"He's lying!" Cameron yelled from behind Bennett. Bennett didn't look at him. He was afraid that if he took his eyes off the dark-haired man, the guy would go for Ivy once more. "You know...Ivy you know I always protect you!"

But...

Did he?

The man before Bennett lifted his hands. "I'll tell you everything, Detective. All our secrets."

Our secrets?

"All our lies…"

Our…

The man laughed again. "All our kills…and dear cousin Cameron planned so many of them—"

"No!" Cameron shouted and then—then Bennett felt a white-hot pain in his back. Fast and deep, cutting through flesh and muscle, sinking into him. It was a familiar pain. One that the Greenville Trapper had made sure he'd never forget.

That bastard Cameron just stabbed a knife into my back.

"*Bennett!*" Ivy screamed. She tried to shove past the dark-haired killer and grab for Bennett, but the man's hands flew out and locked around Ivy. He caught her around the waist even as his other hand flew out and twisted her wrist, squeezing it so that she was forced to drop her knife. The butcher knife clattered down the stairs as Ivy struggled against him. She dropped her body, yanking down hard in an attempt to force her freedom.

And when she dropped, Bennett fired his gun. The bullet flew right toward the dark-haired SOB. It sank into his chest. The guy's mouth opened in shock, then he slumped down on Ivy.

Bennett wanted to whirl and fire at Cameron. The traitorous jerk was behind him. He'd yanked the knife out of Bennett's back and he was —

Cameron put the blade to Bennett's throat. "Drop the gun, *now*."

Bennett didn't drop his weapon. If he did that, then Cameron would slice open his jugular. And while Bennett bled out, Cameron would attack Ivy.

Not happening.

Ivy shoved the other man off her. He fell in a heap, sagging against the stair railing. His eyes were closed. Blood covered his chest. Bennett thought he'd hit the guy's heart, but he couldn't be sure.

"Drop the gun," Cameron said.

The fool had made a mistake. He'd stopped to give orders. He should have just tried to cut Bennett's throat when he had the chance. Cameron thought that Bennett valued his own life — more than anything else. That the threat of death would work to control him.

So wrong.

Ivy mattered more to him than his own life.

In the distance, he could hear the shriek of police sirens. They wouldn't get there in time, though, not in time to stop him.

Bennett smiled at Ivy. He knew he'd have to move fast. And he knew that Cameron might cut him too deep. It was a risk he had to take.

Another psycho with a knife...story of my life.

But he wasn't scared of this psycho. He was just pissed.

Ivy was crouched on the stairs. She shook her head as she gazed up at him. "Bennett..."

I love you.

Then — in a lightning fast move — Bennett twisted his wrist, aiming the gun *behind* him, and he fired back as fast as he could, pulling the trigger on his weapon. He could feel the burn of the bullet slide past his own side as it flew back and sank deep into Cameron's stomach.

Cameron grunted at the impact, and then his knife sliced across Bennett's throat as he stumbled back. But Bennett was already moving, too, spinning around fast so the blade barely nicked the surface of his skin. Bennett brought his gun up. He aimed it right between Cameron's eyes.

Cameron dropped the knife. He staggered, falling down to the bottom of the stairs as he grabbed his stomach. "You...you shot me!"

Hell, yes, he had.

Cameron curled up even more. His face was chalk white and his eyes burned with hate.

"*Ivy!*" Bennett desperately called her name. He needed to touch her. To hold her. But he wasn't taking his aim off Cameron. He had the feeling that sick jerk was just waiting for a weak moment so he could attack again.

But then she was there. Wrapping her arms around his stomach. Holding tight. Warm. Soft. *Alive.*

"No!" Cameron yelled. "No, she doesn't go back to you!" He straightened up, but kept one hand over his bleeding gut. "Not after all I did..."

"All of those women," Bennett said because he'd figured it out. "They were her, weren't they? Only it wasn't just one killer hunting..." Now it made sense to him. Two different cities...two different killers. One in New Orleans. One in Mobile.

And the victims...the women...*all with dark hair like Ivy.*

"Cameron?" Ivy's voice shook with shock.

Cameron's face hardened. "You're the one who looked so good in blood. Remember that day at your...your grandfather's old PI office? That guy with the knife had cut you...you bled and bled...so beautiful."

Bennett felt Ivy tremble beside him.

The sirens were louder. The other cops would be there soon. The nightmare would be over.

With more bodies left to bury.

"I killed for you," Cameron said as he gazed up at Ivy. "You hated your father. He was always in your way. Always controlling you. I told him that I would take care of you, that he could step back, and you know what he said? *To me?*"

Bennett wanted to pull the trigger more than he wanted his next breath.

I'm the cop. I'm supposed to hold back.

But...

That bastard had hurt Ivy.

"Your drunken ass of a father told me I wasn't good enough for you. That I couldn't have *you*." Cameron's stare cut to Bennett. He smiled. "I was better than him. I hadn't left you. I never would. So I just...I eliminated the problem between us."

"You shot my father," Ivy whispered.

"I put him out of his misery!" Brutal words.

"And all those women?" Bennett asked him, sickened. "Did you put them out of their misery, too?" He had a feeling there were so many dead bodies out there, courtesy of Cameron.

Cameron's face hardened. "I killed the first one when Ivy told me our night together had been a 'mistake', that it wouldn't happen again. Because we were such good *friends*."

"You sonofabitch." Ivy took a step toward Cameron. "I didn't love you. I never loved you. I loved Bennett! It was always him!"

"No!" Cameron shook his head. Hard. "He didn't love you! He screwed with your head. It was me, it was—" He lunged toward her.

Bennett shoved Ivy to the side and he fired his weapon.

Cameron's body fell back.

"It wasn't you," Bennett said flatly. "Not even close, asshole."

Ivy glanced back at him. He could feel the blood pooling down his back, and his knees were getting weak. He threw out a hand, holding onto the banister, even as he kept his gun pointed at Cameron. The guy was still breathing, so that meant Cameron was a threat.

One I need to end.

"Go unlock the front door, Ivy," Bennett said. *I want her away from Cameron.* "The other cops will be pulling up any moment." *This will all be over.*

"How badly are you hurt?" Ivy asked him.

"Not enough to kill me." He'd make that a promise. "Get the door, baby, please…" Because he didn't want her to see what would happen next. He'd rather Ivy not remember him this way.

She hurried off the stairs, skirted around Cameron, then rushed toward the foyer.

Bennett glanced down at the man slumped on the stairs. The dark-haired fellow who'd called Cameron his cousin.

The man who was glaring at him.

Yeah, I knew you weren't done yet, either.

"You didn't just kill the dark-haired women, did you?" Bennett asked him. "You killed anyone you wanted. *That's* why the councilman was murdered. Cameron liked the women who looked like Ivy, but you just liked killing."

The sick freak smiled at Bennett. "Sounds like..." He heaved out a rough breath. "You know me."

"I do," Bennett said sadly. He knew the man's type exactly. A killer, through and through. A man who now thought he had nothing to lose.

I guess I missed his heart. Maybe because a screwed-up killer like him doesn't have one.

The guy lunged up at Bennett.

He fired. Damn near point blank.

The bastard didn't get up again.

Bennett kept his hold on the banister as he slowly made his way down to the bottom of the stairs. Then he leaned over Cameron, ignoring the pain that radiated from his back and ignoring the blood that dripped off him. He wouldn't have long. Ivy would be back at any moment.

He put the gun to Cameron's head. "She was never for you," he said again.

Cameron's eyes opened. He squinted, staring up at Bennett.

"You think you'll play the crazy card. You think you'll convince a jury that you were manipulated by whoever that dumb fuck was up there on the stairs." Cameron's cousin? Maybe. Bennett didn't care who the guy had been. He knew exactly how this game played out. "You think you'll get sent to some psych ward for a few months, maybe even a few years, but then you'll get out again."

Cameron's lips began to curl.

Bennett pushed the gun down a bit harder. "You won't. I'm not going to let you ever get near her again."

Blood covered Cameron's once perfectly white teeth. "You're the cop. True blue...you can't kill me like this."

Couldn't he? *Without a hesitation.* "You don't know me. For Ivy, I would do anything."

That smile of Cameron's dimmed.

"You won't hurt her again."

He heard the screech of brakes outside. The cops, back-up, finally at the scene. If he wanted to take out Cameron, this was the moment.

"Bennett..."

He stiffened at that voice. Not Ivy's voice. A man's voice, pain-filled.

He kept the gun on Cameron, but Bennett turned his head. There, at the top of the stairs, watching him with wide eyes — *her eyes* — was Hugh. A very bloody but still alive Hugh.

"You're better...than he is," Hugh said.

Bennett wondered just what all Hugh had heard. "I can't let him come after her." And he knew, he *knew* from his time at Violent Crimes that obsessions like Cameron's wouldn't just end with some therapy. The man was too fixated on her. Too lost in Ivy.

It had to end.

He could do it. Right then.

"Don't." And now, that *was* Ivy's voice. His head whipped toward her. She'd rushed back inside, ahead of the cops. She stood just a few feet away. Her eyes were on him. Tears filled her beautiful gaze. "He's done, Bennett. It's over."

Then she ran to him. She took the gun from him and Bennett—he wrapped his arms around her. He held her tight. Just felt her against him—warm and safe and alive.

The cops rushed in. The chief was with them, and the guy swore when he got a look at the scene. Yeah, Bennett was sure the place looked like a real blood bath.

It felt like one.

Bennett tightened his hold on Ivy. "Cameron Wilde...he's a killer. Wounded, but not dead." Unfortunately. *Not yet.* "And the man...on the stairs...that's his accomplice. He's dead." He had to be. Bennett had made sure of that one.

"Get some ambulances in here, *now*," Chief Quarrel ordered as he hurried forward. A whistle slipped from him. "Damn, boy, just what the hell happened here?"

Death.

Two cops in uniform bent over Cameron. "Jesus," one muttered. "Are you sure he's still alive?"

"Yes," Bennett rasped, "be—"

Careful.

Cameron's hand flew up from beneath his body. A knife was gripped in his fist. Small, bloody. He drove that knife into the cop's side and lurched up.

Boom.

That bullet blasted into Cameron's head.

Silence.

Then Cameron crumpled and the cops swarmed.

Ivy still had the gun aimed, but her head turned, and her gaze met Bennett's. There was no regret in her dark stare. No shock. No horror.

Her breath slipped out on a little sigh. "He won't come back again."

No. Neither of them would.

"Sometimes," Ivy said. "The killers don't stop…they keep coming…"

Until death.

He buried his face in the curve of her neck. He inhaled her scent. He *felt* her. Ivy…

Safe. Alive.

The best miracle of his life.

EPILOGUE

There weren't a lot of people at the cemetery. The news crews had already came and left. They'd gotten their thirty second video to show on TV that night.

Ivy stood away from the graves. Two graves, side by side. Her gaze lingered on those graves as she thought about the tragedy that had been caused by the men beneath that dirt.

Cameron Wilde and a man who had actually turned out to be Cameron's cousin, Julian Abbott. Julian had been a New Orleans native. From what Bennett had learned, Julian had been in trouble with the law for years, but his wealthy family had smoothed over much of that drama.

And Cameron...

I never saw the truth. How could she have been so blind?

"Ivy."

Her eyes closed and she shivered. Bennett said her name like no other. Softly, sensually, and, most importantly, with love.

His hands closed around her shoulders. "The cops in New Orleans finished searching

Julian's estate there. They found a diary that
he'd been keeping. He and Cameron — shit, baby,
there were more victims. Victims dating back — "

"Back to the day I made my 'mistake' with
Cameron," she said, pain twisting through her.

Bennett turned her in his arms. "You didn't
do a damn thing." A muscle flexed in his jaw.
"Cameron did it. He's the one who started it
all — Julian wrote that Cameron made the first
kill. They were drinking in New Orleans.
Cameron was at one of the parades over in the
Big Easy with his cousin. They saw a woman
who was perfect. Cameron slept with her, then
he found a Mardi Gras mask at Julian's place. He
found that mask, put it on..."

And she'd died.

"After that..." Bennett exhaled. "Julian
wrote that it became a game for them. All about
power and the thrill. Sometimes, they'd hunt in
Mobile. Sometimes in New Orleans. But
Cameron tried to set up rules, and Julian didn't
like to follow orders. Hell, from what I can tell,
he just liked to kill. So he chose different targets.
He...hell, Ivy, he fits the pattern of a
psychopath. The only person Julian seemed to
care about was Cameron, only Cameron never
told him *why* they were only supposed to kill
brunettes. He never told him about you, not
until the end."

She shivered. "He...Julian lost control,
didn't he?"

"I think he felt like Cameron had been holding back on him. Keeping a secret — *keeping you secret* — only there weren't supposed to be any secrets between them."

Such a twisted pair. "When I saw Julian kill Evette —"

"Cameron set that up. He told Julian when to kill that woman. Told him your float number, told him what side you'd be on. The fucking bastard *wanted* you to see it happen, but I don't think he realized just what chain of events that would set in motion."

A chain of events that led to murder.

"He didn't know you'd jump off that float to save her. Cameron didn't know that Julian would get a good look at you, that he'd start stalking you because he'd realized how much you meant to his cousin...and to their game." Bennett's gaze slipped to the graves. The funeral home had put one spray of flowers on each grave. No other flowers were at the scene. "But their game is over, and they can't hurt anyone now."

No, they couldn't.

"I didn't want that on you." His forehead sagged forward and pressed to hers. "I didn't want you killing Cameron. You should have let me do it."

She'd known he planned that. She'd also known... "Bennett, I carry my own darkness." She put her hand on his chest. "Cameron stabbed you. He wanted *you* dead." She'd shot that bullet not just for herself, but for Bennett. For Hugh. "You're not the only one who knows how to protect the people you love."

His hand covered hers. "I *do* love you. I never stopped."

Neither had she.

His head lifted. He stared down at her with a tender gaze. He'd been patched up, she'd been patched up, and her brother — Hugh was slowly healing. Julian *had* tried to kill him. He'd stabbed her brother five times, but Hugh had survived.

We're all survivors.

They'd survived the madness. They'd beat the monsters.

This time.

"You have to admit," Ivy murmured, "I'm not the worst partner in the world, am I?" She had rather saved the day. At least, she thought so.

Bennett's gaze dropped to her lips. "Not the worst. The damn best...the only one I ever want."

She smiled at him. "Good answer."

Bennett pressed a soft kiss to her lips. "I want to do everything right with you this time." He tucked her hand under his elbow and they walked away from that cemetery. From the monsters that would never hurt anyone again. "Every damn thing. I want you to know what you mean to me."

Ivy just shook her head. They didn't speak again until they were out of that cemetery. Until they were away from the ghosts.

The sun streamed down on them. Bright and warm.

She tilted her head back, just enjoying the moment. Happy to be alive.

"You don't have to prove anything to me," Ivy finally said. "All you have to do…just keep loving me, Bennett. Love me."

Always.

And she would love him.

Through the good times. The bad. Through whatever hell came their way.

No more fear. No more secrets.

Partners.

THE END

###

I hope you enjoyed UNTIL DEATH. If you would like to try another one of my romantic suspense novels, read on for a sneak peek at BEWARE OF ME.

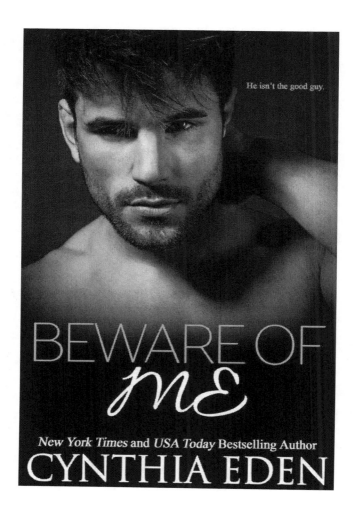

He isn't the good guy.

BEWARE OF
me

New York Times and USA Today Bestselling Author
CYNTHIA EDEN

Walk on the wild side with *New York Times* and *USA Today* best-selling author Cynthia Eden's dark new romantic suspense, BEWARE OF ME.

Criminal. Killer. Monster. Ethan Barclay has been called many things in life, and he usually doesn't care what people say about him. He's tough, hard, and brutal when he needs to be. But even the most dangerous of men can have a weakness. Ethan's weakness has — and always will be — Carly Shay.

Their pasts are tied together — twisted and melded by blood and death. Walking away from Carly was the hardest thing that Ethan ever did, but it was also his one good deed. He knew Carly deserved far better than him, and he wanted her to have a perfect life, a life that didn't involve paying for Ethan's sins.

Only now the secrets from their past have been revealed, and Carly's life is on the line. Ethan's enemies, Carly's enemies — the predators are closing in on them. But Ethan isn't going to let Carly be threatened. He will move heaven and hell to protect her. He won't lose Carly, not again, and for those foolish enough to try and take her from him…they are about to see just how deadly Ethan truly can be.

BEWARE OF ME
CHAPTER ONE EXCERPT

Carly Shay hurried up the subway steps, her high heels making the climb feel far more difficult than it should. People jostled around her, moving quickly, but she kept pace with them. After all, she'd been living in New York for years. She knew this town. Knew this place inside and out.

The crowds — the wonderful energy — she could disappear in this city. Blend in easily. And no one gave her a second glance.

That was why she'd first come to New York. To vanish in the crowd. To stop attracting attention. The way Carly figured it, she'd done a damn good job of vanishing.

One hand kept a firm grip on her bag as she marched forward and across the street. A few more minutes, and she'd be home free.

"Carly."

She almost slammed into him. She'd been focused on the crowd. On the guy in the fancy suit who was yelling into his phone. On the mother trying to comfort her crying toddler.

She hadn't even seen *him*.

But now, she couldn't look anywhere else.

Because in the middle of the sidewalk, standing less than three feet from her, was the man who haunted far too many of her dreams. Well, her nightmares really.

Ethan Barclay.

Tall, dark, and far too dangerous to know…Ethan Barclay.

The dying sunlight fell on his dark hair. Hair that was a little too long. Dark stubble covered his jaw and his golden eyes — tiger eyes — were locked on her with the full intensity of a predator who'd just found the perfect prey.

I won't be his prey. Not this time.

"You left D.C. without saying good-bye," Ethan told her. His hands were shoved deeply into the pockets of his coat, and that coat stretched across his broad shoulders. *Powerful.* Yes, she knew Ethan was incredibly strong. He wasn't the twenty-one-year-old boy she'd known so long ago.

He was a man now. A stranger. One who was reputed to be far more dangerous than Quincy Atkins had ever been.

When Quincy vanished, Ethan took over D.C. And…

Carly had tried to pick up the pieces of her life.

Even though it was warm for New York at that time of the year, a shiver slid over Carly. "I...I was only back in D.C. to check on my stepsister."

"Um..." His voice was a low, deep rumble and he was closing in on her. Eliminating that space between them as he stalked closer. Someone jostled her from behind, but before Carly could stumble, Ethan's hands — big, strong, but oddly gentle as they held her — curled around her shoulders. "Back in D.C. long enough to save Julianna's life...and get shot."

She'd been shot twice, actually. But it had been worth it. Julianna had been put at risk because she'd been trying to protect Carly — and the crimes from Carly's past. *Quincy's murder.* "I wasn't going to let Julianna be hurt again because of me."

His eyelashes flickered. Long eyelashes. They should have looked ridiculous on a man like him, but they didn't. They just made his intense eyes appear all the...sexier. Dammit. She shouldn't find him sexy. Not at all. She should have moved way, way beyond him by this point.

The way he'd moved beyond her.

"I thought you were going to die." His voice was rough as he made that confession. Ragged around the edges. Very much *not* Ethan.

You don't know him any longer. You probably never knew him — not the real guy.

"You were bleeding out on the floor of that apartment," Ethan said, as his hold tightened on her. "And during the ambulance ride to the hospital, shit, you left me."

She stilled. "I didn't know you were in the ambulance with me." *And I left him? What does that mean?* No one had said anything about her paying some visit to the afterlife. Maybe the EMTs didn't share that info with her though because they might have realized...*it freaks me out.*

"I was in the ambulance," he told her grimly. "And at your hospital bedside, until I realized that I was a threat to you."

Carly had to swallow to ease the growing lump in her throat. *You're always a threat to me.*

"But I left too late, and now others know..."

"Okay, Ethan, I really don't get why you're in New York, but we don't have anything to discuss." Did her voice sound cool? Dismissive? Probably not, but she'd really been aiming for that tone. "Now let me go because I want to get home." It had been her first day back at her job since she'd been shot and she was exhausted. It took all of her strength not to show that weakness to him, but she knew that if he realized how close to trembling she was...the guy would pounce.

"You know why I'm in New York." He didn't let her go. In fact, he seemed to inch even closer. Because Ethan was a big guy, well over six feet, she had to tip back her head as she gazed up at him. Even in heels, she didn't come close to his height. "I'm here for you."

Once, she'd longed to hear him say those words. When she'd been a terrified teenager, when she hadn't been able to deal with the guilt and shame and horror of what had happened to her...she'd longed for him. She'd broken, her whole world imploding when her father had passed away so closely behind her attack by Quincy.

And a psych ward had become her home when she'd lost control.

I screamed for Ethan. But Ethan hadn't been there. "Let's be clear on a few things." She kept her body stiff in his hold. "Our relationship is over. Long over." As in...*years* over. "It ended one blood-soaked night when you put me in a cab and just walked away from me. You didn't contact me again...you didn't so much as call me. You built up your life and you moved the hell on." Now she jerked back, tearing out of his hands because she didn't want his touch. It made her remember too much about the past. "And now, so have I. Just because I returned to D.C. to help my *sister,* that did not mean that I went back for you."

His eyes glittered with emotion.

"Now get out of my way, Ethan. Because we're done."

His blazing stare raked over her. "How many secrets do you carry?"

A NOTE FROM THE AUTHOR

Thanks so much for taking the time to read UNTIL DEATH. I hope you enjoyed the story!

I grew up in Mobile, Alabama, and Mardi Gras was always a city-wide event that swept everyone away in a wave of excitement. I've always loved Mardi Gras (only without serial killers!), and it was great to have the opportunity to write about a city and event so near to my heart.

If you'd like to stay updated on my releases and sales, please join my newsletter list www.cynthiaeden.com/newsletter/. You can also check out my Facebook page www.facebook.com/cynthiaedenfanpage. I love to post giveaways over at Facebook!

Again, thank you for reading UNTIL DEATH.

Best,
Cynthia Eden
www.cynthiaeden.com

ABOUT THE AUTHOR

Award-winning author Cynthia Eden writes dark tales of paranormal romance and romantic suspense. She is a *New York Times, USA Today, Digital Book World,* and *IndieReader* best-seller. Cynthia is also a three-time finalist for the RITA® award. Since she began writing full-time in 2005, Cynthia has written over fifty novels and novellas.

Cynthia is a southern girl who loves horror movies, chocolate, and happy endings. More information about Cynthia and her books may be found at: http://www.cynthiaeden.com or on her Facebook page at: http://www.facebook.com/cynthiaedenfanpage . Cynthia is also on Twitter at http://www.twitter.com/cynthiaeden.

HER WORKS

List of Cynthia Eden's romantic suspense titles:
- WATCH ME (Dark Obsession, Book 1)
- WANT ME (Dark Obsession, Book 2)
- NEED ME (Dark Obsession, Book 3)
- MINE TO TAKE (Mine, Book 1)
- MINE TO KEEP (Mine, Book 2)
- MINE TO HOLD (Mine, Book 3)
- MINE TO CRAVE (Mine, Book 4)
- MINE TO HAVE (Mine, Book 5)
- FIRST TASTE OF DARKNESS
- SINFUL SECRETS
- DIE FOR ME (For Me, Book 1)
- FEAR FOR ME (For Me, Book 2)
- SCREAM FOR ME (For Me, Book 3)
- DEADLY FEAR (Deadly, Book 1)
- DEADLY HEAT (Deadly, Book 2)
- DEADLY LIES (Deadly, Book 3)
- ALPHA ONE (Shadow Agents, Book 1)
- GUARDIAN RANGER (Shadow Agents, Book 2)
- SHARPSHOOTER (Shadow Agents, Book 3)

- GLITTER AND GUNFIRE (Shadow Agents, Book 4)
- UNDERCOVER CAPTOR (Shadow Agents, Book 5)
- THE GIRL NEXT DOOR (Shadow Agents, Book 6)
- EVIDENCE OF PASSION (Shadow Agents, Book 7)
- WAY OF THE SHADOWS (Shadow Agents, Book 8)

Paranormal romances by Cynthia Eden:
- BOUND BY BLOOD (Bound, Book 1)
- BOUND IN DARKNESS (Bound, Book 2)
- BOUND IN SIN (Bound, Book 3)
- BOUND BY THE NIGHT (Bound, Book 4)
- *FOREVER BOUND - An anthology containing: BOUND BY BLOOD, BOUND IN DARKNESS, BOUND IN SIN, AND BOUND BY THE NIGHT
- BOUND IN DEATH (Bound, Book 5)
- THE WOLF WITHIN (Purgatory, Book 1)
- MARKED BY THE VAMPIRE (Purgatory, Book 2)
- CHARMING THE BEAST (Purgatory, Book 3) - Available October 2014

Other paranormal romances by Cynthia Eden:
- A VAMPIRE'S CHRISTMAS CAROL
- BLEED FOR ME
- BURN FOR ME (Phoenix Fire, Book 1)

- ONCE BITTEN, TWICE BURNED (Phoenix Fire, Book 2)
- PLAYING WITH FIRE (Phoenix Fire, Book 3)
- ANGEL OF DARKNESS (Fallen, Book 1)
- ANGEL BETRAYED (Fallen, Book 2)
- ANGEL IN CHAINS (Fallen, Book 3)
- AVENGING ANGEL (Fallen, Book 4)
- IMMORTAL DANGER
- NEVER CRY WOLF
- A BIT OF BITE (Free Read!!)
- ETERNAL HUNTER (Night Watch, Book 1)
- I'LL BE SLAYING YOU (Night Watch, Book 2)
- ETERNAL FLAME (Night Watch, Book 3)
- HOTTER AFTER MIDNIGHT (Midnight, Book 1)
- MIDNIGHT SINS (Midnight, Book 2)
- MIDNIGHT'S MASTER (Midnight, Book 3)
- WHEN HE WAS BAD (anthology)
- EVERLASTING BAD BOYS (anthology)
- BELONG TO THE NIGHT (anthology)